Pizza Dragon
Vegetarian Supreme with Extra Cheese

Joseph R. Lallo

Heart Ally Books, LLC
Camano Island, Washington

Published by:
Heart Ally Books, LLC
heartallybooks.com
26910 92nd Ave NW C5-406, Stanwood, WA 98292
Published on Camano Island, WA, USA

ISBN-13: 978-1-63107-069-3 (epub)
ISBN-13: 978-1-63107-068-6 (paperback)
10 9 8 7 6 5 4 3 2 1

Table of Contents

List of Illustrations

Blodgette Signing "I love you" illustrated by Merri Monster

Author's Introduction

There are few tales that have had a more interesting route to publication than that of the Pizza Dragon. Let's start at the beginning. Many years ago, a talented artist and animator who goes by the name ProjectEndo shared a detailed and fascinating art piece detailing the biology of an original species called *Structophis gastrignae*, more popularly known as the Pizza Dragon. I found the concept to be genuinely intriguing, and as a gift to the creator I wrote a single chapter teaser playing with the concept. In time it grew into an entire novel, which Endo graciously allowed me to publish. That initial release went under the name *Structophis*, a title which remains available. But the story doesn't end there. Oh no.

Alongside my author career, I've also spent time as a book marketing podcaster, and in the years since its release, *Structophis* has been something of a case study in difficulty in marketing. I made nearly every mistake with that first release. Hard to spell and hard to remember name? Check. Off-the-wall premise? Check. Uncertain genre? Check. But despite me fumbling every aspect of the release, the story has developed a small and dedicated following. And when folks like a story, I try to give them more. The first tasty nugget came in the form of a small prequel story given to my newsletter subscribers, *The Eggs of the Abbey*. When that wasn't enough to satisfy the Pizza Dragon fans, I gave them a nice little epilogue story called *Blodgette's Big Day*. Folks liked both tales, and that seemed like it would be the end of it.

But it was not.

For one, there was no easy way to get your hands on *all* of these stories. Indeed, *The Eggs of the Abbey* is downright difficult to dig up. And then there's the fact that a certain fan of the series just so happened to have a publishing imprint. Having seen the errors in my ways, she became convinced that a little tender loving care could give Pizza Dragon a new life. I was more than willing to give her the chance to try. You are now reading the result.

Pizza Dragon: Vegetarian Supreme with Extra Cheese is a super-sized edition, featuring all of the words written for the series, as well as all original art pieces produced for it as well. I hope you enjoy it. It's been a wild ride!

-Joseph Lallo

Chapter 1

Markus had only just flopped onto his couch and pulled out his tablet for the first bit of nonacademic reading in… long enough that he couldn't remember how long it was. A full-time job as a veterinary tech would have been plenty to keep him busy. But lately he'd begun to feel as though tending to the pampered pets of the local ski towns wasn't as fulfilling and valuable to society as he would like, so he'd returned to college via night classes. It had all left him stretched a little thin. Unwinding with something that included damsels and/or spaceships sounded like a long overdue balm for his frazzled brain, and a half day at the job meant he had time for it before lunch and studying. Perhaps inevitably, a ringing phone brought the whole endeavor to a screeching halt. And it was *just* when he'd reached the first instance of the word "forsooth," too.

He fumbled for the *other* glass-and-plastic rectangle that dominated his life and swiped the screen.

"Hello?" he muttered, endeavoring to imbue the word with the proper tone for it to convey the subtext, you are interrupting the only fifteen-minute period of my week not otherwise earmarked for thinking about or working with sick animals; please be brief.

"Markus?" said a voice on the other end.

He flinched. It was Aunt Sabina. This was not going to be a short call… The woman didn't speak in sentences, she spoke in cycles. If you ever missed something you just had to wait for it to come around again.

"Do you remember your Great Uncle Dimitrios?" she said.

"Yeah, I remember him. I spent a couple of years working in his restaurant."

"He always used to shovel coal into that big gas deck oven in the back," she continued, as though he hadn't spoken.

"Yes, Aunt Beeni. I was the one doing the shoveling."

"He was the one with the curly mustache and he always had egg stains on his shirt—"

"Yes! Yes. I remember Great Uncle Dimitrios," he barked impatiently.

"Well, he's dead."

"...What?"

"Yeah... or left on a trip. I don't know. It's not important."

"... Aunt Beeni, I submit that 'dead' versus 'on a trip' is in fact a *very* important distinction."

"Well, you know Dimitrios. Always the impulsive type. You remember him, don't you? He was the—"

"Beeni, I don't mean to rush you, but did you call for a reason besides giving me the most unsettling family update imaginable?"

"Do you still have the key to the back room to his bistro?"

"Probably, somewhere."

"Good. You need to go down there and shut off the oven. He's been gone for days and the nice old lady in the apartment upstairs says she smells something burning. Dimitrios still has you as the emergency contact. He's got a note here that says 'Don't let anyone but Markus tend to the special oven.'"

Markus twisted his face a bit. Slowly, like a pile of junk teetering forward out of the recently opened door of a long-forgotten closet, a rush of memories slammed into him. He remembered "the special oven," and he remembered it with the very specific level of clarity reserved for things one has tried countless times to forget.

"Uh... You're... *sure* I'm the one who has to do it? I haven't been down there in like... five years," he said, adding in his head, *I know, because that's when the nightmares started.*

"It's that or someone breaks the door down. The lady upstairs says something's burning. And she's been hearing scratching. Probably rats. You know Dimitrios... Do you—"

"Yes, I remember Dimitrios. I'll be there in a half hour. Bye, Aunt Sabina."

He ended the call before she could go through another iteration and hopped to his feet, grabbing his car keys. After a steadying breath, he opened the closet and pushed aside a few old coats until he unearthed a soot-stained Dimitrios's Deluxe Delivery jacket. A bit of fumbling through the pockets unearthed a key. He held it as if it was liable to explode at any moment.

"Okay, Markus. You can do this. There's no *way* it's as bad as you remember."

***

Markus pushed open the staff entrance at the rear of Dimitrios's Bistro. A very unique, very intense scent struck him immediately. It smelled like char. Not any specific *type* of char, mind you. If anything, it was representative of the whole pizza-kitchen section of the char spectrum. There were overtones of charred oregano, some heavy charred flour smells, a little chunk charcoal, the spicy sting of charred red pepper, and the bright tinge of charred tomato.

"Okay, so the lady upstairs wasn't crazy about the burning smell," he said to himself.

A long, grating grind and the plink of metal rumbled out from deep within a back room, startling him enough to bash his head on the edge of the still-open door.

"Darn it," he said, rubbing his head. "So the sound wasn't her imagination either."

He shut the door and found the light switch, revealing a scene that brought back an almost dizzying rush of memories.

Everything looked precisely as it had in the nineteen sixties. That wouldn't have been impressive if it had *closed* in the sixties, but the place had been open as recently as the previous Monday. Dimitrios was... distrustful of change. Everything was covered in either linoleum or Naugahyde, then topped with a generous layer of soot.

"Still?" Markus said, running his finger across a countertop to clear a line of the black dust that accumulated on every available surface.

Technically the place cooked all its food in gas ovens, but Uncle Dimitrios always kept a few sacks of natural charcoal to shovel into his "special" oven in the back room. That "privilege" had always been Markus's, despite the fact that he'd never been entrusted with what exactly it was that made the oven so darn special. As best as he could remember, there were only three things about it that made it any different from the other ovens.

The first difference was, rather than just stacking two deck ovens, Uncle Dimitrios had gotten all "junkyard wars" with it. He'd carved out the bottom of one oven and the top of another, then welded them together into one big, hollow monstrosity. The second difference was that he'd disconnected and sealed off the gas lines, deciding for some insane reason that it was a better idea to feed the contraption with good old-fashioned charcoal. Manning the shovel was sweltering and dirty work, to say nothing of the work of cleaning out the dust afterward.

Markus wouldn't have minded all the shoveling... No, that would be overstating it. He would have *understood* all the shoveling if they had ever pulled any pizza out of the oven. But as far as he could tell, nothing at all ever came out of that oven.

He stepped up to the door to the room Dimitrios had set aside for the special oven, and hesitated. That, of course, was the third thing about the oven. Markus had worked for his great uncle for the better part of five years, from when he was fifteen until he was almost twenty. One of the first jobs he'd been given was feeding the special oven, a task that had a very long and very precise sequence of requirements and instructions. Don't keep the door open too long, only use the chunk charcoal, be careful about the big round chunk in the middle...

Eventually his uncle must have changed his mind about the big chunk, because one day Markus had opened the oven and found that someone had removed it and tossed in a wad of dough. It had always sort of made Markus uneasy that his uncle evidently threw a new wad in every morning and despite baking all day, it never seemed to get any more "done." His uneasiness compounded over the years when the dough began to look... organic. There were recognizable bits. An arm here, a leg there. At the time he'd assumed his uncle was just experimenting with sculpture and was too cheap to buy a kiln. By the end of the third year though, his uneasiness had escalated to full weirded-out status. It was around that time a hunk of coal with a smoldering red center had gotten lodged in the dough/clay thing in a way that was a little too eyelike for his tastes.

By that time he had been eighteen and should have known better, but he could *have sworn* the thing was watching him, gazing as he opened the lower deck door to sweep out the spent powder and blinking up at him when he dropped the fresh stuff in the top door. It had sent shivers down his spine every time he'd seen it, but he'd stuck with it because Dimitrios had insisted it was the most important part of his job, and the old man simply didn't trust any of the other delivery boys to do it.

The last straw had been when he'd tended to the oven one morning, pulling it open to brush it out, and he was certain the thing had crawled toward him. He'd quit that day, and hadn't been back since. As far as he was concerned, there were only two possible explanations for that. The first was that he was going insane, and the second was that there was some sort of gremlin living in an oven in the back of Dimitrios's Bistro. Neither potential truth appealed to him, so he'd opted for the very popular let-us-never-speak-of-this-again approach, which had worked fairly well until Aunt Beeni called.

"Maybe… maybe I can just leave it. The darn oven's going to have to burn itself out eventually with no one to load it. What's the worst that could—"

He was interrupted by another grinding plink, then the unmistakable splash of water and an awful hissing noise. He took a step back as he noticed water rush from under the door and pool around his feet.

"Frickin' great. A pipe burst," he said, hastily fitting the key into the lock. "I've at least got to get the main valve shut off."

He muscled the door open and splashed inside the back room, eyes sweeping the floor for any electrical wires that might be in the water waiting to put him in an early grave. Dimitrios was one of those guys who cut the "fat peg" off power cords because "they only get in the way." It didn't give one a warm feeling about the survivability of a flooded back room.

When Markus finally glanced up, now in search of the source of the trickling water, the possibility of electrocution was suddenly a distant third on his priorities list. The first was his sanity, and the second was the thing that would likely kill him in the event he *wasn't* insane.

It was… a *thing*. That was as good a place as any to start. It was standing on two things that could certainly be called "feet," though "paws" seemed more appropriate. They were pudgy little footsies, a dark, crackly brown color like baked dough. The feet disappeared up into what had probably been chunks of the old oven, but it had seen better days. The front, back, and sides had all split in a number of places, roughly in equal lines that allowed them to bow out. From between these cracks more of the crusty hide could be seen, though some of them also revealed a deep orange glow. Some hunks of metal were pulled entirely away from the others, revealing a massive potbelly of the same dark, crackly texture. In the cracks on the skin, a dull glow was again visible. The way the plates and doors that had formerly made up the oven hung at blocky angles put Markus in mind of an old samurai warrior's armor.

Overall the... *thing* that had grown out of the oven was a bit bigger than the oven itself, and it had only slightly changed its shape. Two pudgy arms, very stout and ending in smallish hands with stubby little fingers, had emerged from the sides, wearing the strips of oven punched free when the arms emerged as a sort of half-gauntlet/extended brass knuckles. The roof of the oven sloped upward slightly along the creature's metal-clad shoulders, giving way to a long, crooked neck that was topped by a rather organically sculpted helmet of sorts that kept a bit of the samurai mojo present in the rest of the ensemble. There was a somewhat more forward-jutting snout than one might see on a samurai mask, but the top of it had the angular sloping shape that fit the bill nicely, and even antlerish metal horns that seemed to continue that aesthetic.

Behind it a crooked, kinked tail with a cruel-looking metal spade formed on to its end emerged from the back of the former stove. The jagged zigzag shape of the tail made it seem as if it had been pinned up against the wall of the oven until the day it had burst free, maintaining the creases it had earned during that time. Nevertheless, the tail was pudgy and bulky, almost as large as the rest of its body combined.

Currently the thing had its head tipped up to the sprinkler system, guzzling the flow of water out of a pipe it had punctured, like some sort of overgrown hamster slurping from a water dispenser.

"Whuuaaaaahua?" Markus said.

That was the most intelligent comment his brain could muster on short notice.

The utterance did the job, evidently, because as soon as he made the outburst the creature looked to him, eyes glowing through slits in the mask. It tipped its head to the side, releasing a rolling grumble. It didn't *sound* violent or threatening, but he felt it was probably best to take the "T-Rex" approach and hold perfectly still. *Jurassic Park* had yet to steer him wrong.

At this point, for the sake of some degree of specificity, Markus's brain resolved to label this thing a "dragon." The dragon waddled up to him, its body clinking considerably less than he would have expected, and leaned its head close. Thanks to the hunched-over fold in its neck, it was about the same height as him. Its breath, which swirled from two nostrilesque slits in the mask, was *quite* hot. Nothing in its body language seemed hostile. If anything, the squinting eyes and tipping head were more indicative of confusion. The holding-still thing was therefore a success, and Markus wasn't going to push his luck with any last-minute tactics changes.

Once again, pay dirt. The dragon glanced aside, then shuffled back and rummaged through a pile of old, sooty cloth. Its chubby mitts came up with an old delivery shirt and a coal shovel. Markus was fiddling behind him, trying to surreptitiously open the door and make his escape, but he once again froze when the dragon turned in his direction.

It stopped in front of him again and held up the delivery shirt, pressing it to Markus's front like someone testing an off-the-rack outfit at a department store. Markus felt the handle of the shovel being shoved against his hand. Out of habit, he grabbed it. The dragon then backed away, leaving Markus to obligingly hold the delivery shirt in place as well. After a few moments of tipping its head side to side again, a new look came to its remarkably expressive eyes. A look of recognition.

Markus cringed and shut his eyes as it lunged toward him. An almost-scalding heat pressed against him from the front, and a yielding crunch crackled around him. When he didn't burst into flames and stubbornly refused to be torn to shreds, he ventured a peek through squinted eyes. It took his brain a few seconds to register it, but the thing was—and there was really no other word for it—*hugging* him. It uttered a contented little *murr*, and the reasoning portion of Markus's brain dusted itself off to put the pieces together.

This... this was the thing in the oven. This was the thing he'd fed every morning and cleaned up after every night. For five long years he'd been this thing's keeper, even if he wouldn't allow himself to accept it at the time. And it remembered him. It had *imprinted* on him.

The dragon released him and shuffled back to the leaky pipe to drink some more, and for the moment the spine-tingling terror dropped away enough for Markus's veterinary mind to say a few words. He didn't know the first thing about this creature, but the way the skin was black, brown, and crackling when it moved didn't seem healthy. And if Dimitrios had been gone for a few days, it hadn't been fed, or at least hadn't been given any proper care since then. Its overall proportions didn't seem right, either. The body structure suggested something that should be longer, leaner. Its squat square build looked like the consequence of a mishandled upbringing rather than proper development.

This thing, whatever it was, needed help. It needed looking after. When it turned to him, he glanced down at the center of its chest, where the logo of the original oven manufacturer hung like a name tag. Blodgett.

Markus sighed. "So... Blodgett. You're going to make my life an awful lot more complicated, aren't you...?"

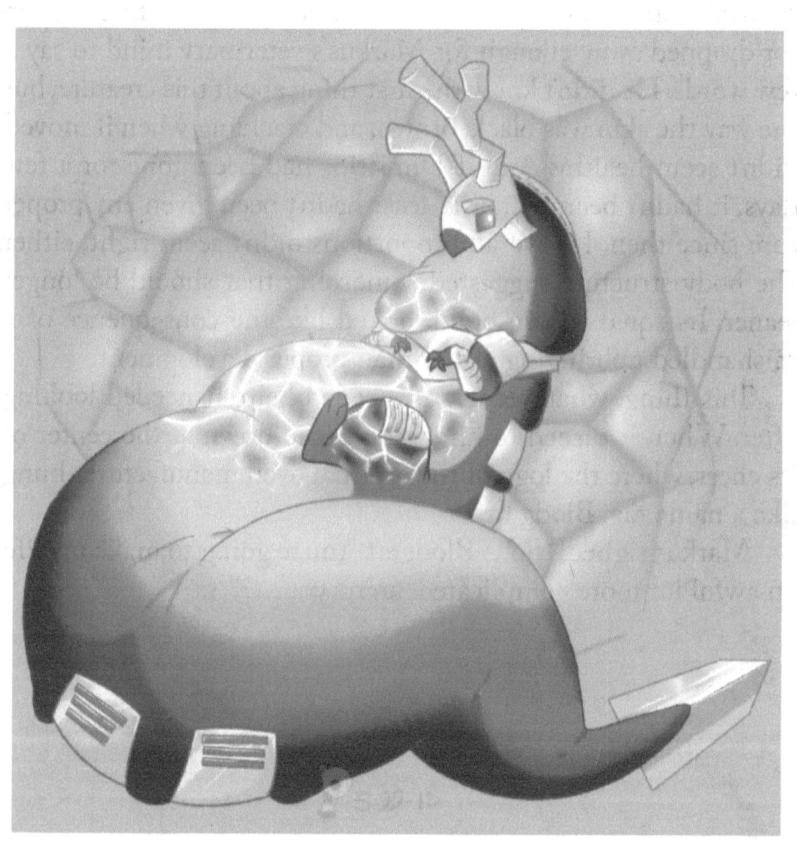

Young Blodgette illustrated by Pandamun

Chapter 2

Markus cast a worried glance out the front windows of the bistro, then finished taping the front curtains shut with a roll of painter's tape he'd found. That job done, he dusted off his hands and dug out his phone.

"Okay…" he said nervously, glancing into the back room, where Blodgett was watching expectantly from the doorway. "I must have her number in here somewhere… Gale, Gale… Where is it?"

Blodgett released an inquisitive, burbling chirp of a sort and stuck its head out through the door to the back room, a.k.a. its nest. Like its tail, Blodgett's neck was shorter than it probably should be, kinked somewhat along its length. Stretching out to see what Markus was up to straightened these kinks a tad, but even as far as they could go, the creature had a disproportionately squat appearance.

It peered side to side, perhaps curious whom Markus was talking to. When it couldn't find anyone else, it leaned against the doorway to get a better look. The doorway, it turned out, was not quite up to the task of supporting the creature. A worrisome crackling and splintering filled the air.

"No, no, no, no! Back, back! It's fine. Don't worry, nothing to see here. Just… go destroy more of the sprinkler system," Markus said in a panic.

Something he said must have sunk in, because Blodgett pulled back into the room, eyeing the damaged doorway distrustfully and nudging it with a pudgy finger.

Markus turned back to his phone. "Let's see... Oh, right!" He flipped back through his contacts until he found the entry he was looking for: *School Contacts—Glasses Girl*. He tapped it and put the phone to his ear.

"Answer... Come on... Come on, *answer*," he muttered, watching Blodgett as Blodgett watched him.

"Hello?" came a wary voice when the call finally connected.

"Gale? Gale Dekker?" Markus said.

"Yes? To whom am I speaking?" she said, still clearly unsure.

"This is Markus."

"Markus..."

"Markus Spiros. From college?"

"Oh... *Oh*... Sorry, Markus, new phone. Didn't have your number in it. So where have you been? Haven't had a class with you in like three semesters, right?"

"Yeah. I was going fairly vocational with my training. You went more research, right?"

"Heh, *of course*," she said, as though he'd asked if she still breathed oxygen. "That's where the action is, Mark my friend. So what's up?"

"Did you, by chance, register for that Exotic Megafauna class they were offering last semester?"

"You *know* it! Best class in the whole curriculum."

"Great. Yes. I thought so. Listen, they didn't, by chance, cover the uh... hang on... I was looking it up before... Struc... Structophis... dragon thing?"

"*Structophis gastrignae?* Of course they did. My third common exam was all about them. Hottest research area in zoology and biology today." She snorted. "No pun intended."

"Right, right. You wouldn't happen to—*no! No! Leave it!*" he blurted.

Blodgett had started to tug at the door frame it had loosened. When Markus yelled, it froze and looked at him but notably did not release the splintered wood.

"Is something wrong, Mark?" Gale asked.

"No. No, it's just—I'm watching my neighbor's dog," he looked pointedly at Blodgett, "and it hasn't learned to behave."

"Oh."

"Anyway. What I wanted to know is if you could recommend any good resources for the Structophis... guh..."

"Structophis gastrignae."

"Right. I was looking online, and there's not a whole lot of reliable info."

"There never is. Sure, I can give you the names of some decent texts. It makes for good reading. Fascinating creatures. Though if you're looking to get into researching them, I'd recommend you save yourself the heartache. I've been trying to get some lab time with one for the past eight months..."

"Yeah, that's great. If you could just give me those textbook titles..." Markus urged, eyes widening as Blodgett turned its attentions back to the door frame.

"... and the waiting list is as long as your arm. We've got *maybe* eighteen hundred in the country. Of those, about four hundred are in subspecies that aren't cleared for academic study, another four hundred are pre-emergence, which makes them no good for study, and the rest are pretty much all on the coasts. You know how many of them are in a flyover state like Colorado?"

"I really don't know, Gale, but if you could just give me names of those books—"

"Zero, Mark. Zero. If you want to get within even a hundred feet of an emerged *Structophis gastrignae*, you're going to have to hop a plane to Washington and wait a good three months, if you're *lucky*."

"Gale, could you—*WHAT DID I SAY?!*"

It was too late. Blodgett had wrapped a crusty mitt around the door frame and given it a good hard yank, easily tearing the wood free. It clutched the broken wood like a toddler with a new toy. Clearly delighted with itself, it shouldered its way through the widened doorway, making it significantly wider in the process. It tromped up to Markus, shaking the floor and pushing tables aside along the way.

"What the heck was that, Mark?" Gale asked.

"Uh… The dog is making a mess."

"Must be a heck of a dog."

Markus looked Blodgett in the eye as it tipped its head and glanced at the phone. "Yeah. It's a very large, very *disobedient* dog."

"So anyway, let me see if I've still got my old textbooks somewhere."

Blodgett, now near enough to hear the tiny voice coming from the phone, twisted its head to the side and tried to wedge it between Markus's face and the phone.

"Cut it out," he whispered through clenched teeth.

The creature chirped something in reply and plodded back toward the rear of the bistro.

"Right, so, as I was saying, maybe—"

"What was that noise?" Gale asked. Her tone suggested she already knew the answer.

"A… pigeon?"

"A pigeon. That's funny, Mark, because it sounded *exactly* like the warbling of an adolescent *Structophis gastrignae*."

"It's a really big pigeon."

"Where are you? I'm coming over."

"No, no, I just need the textbooks."

"Yeah, fine. I'll bring the textbooks when I come over. Where are you?"

"Honest, I just need the *names* so I can—"

"What? Order them from Amazon? They don't make these big, fat biology texts as e-books, pal. You're going to have to go hardcopy and get it delivered. What're you going to do in the meantime? Just observe? From the sounds of it, you've got your hands full. I was planning a *thesis* on the *Structophis gastrignae*. You can't even say it."

Blodgette investigated, then dislodged, a shelf of condiments.

"Oh, great. Red pepper flakes everywhere. Wonderful," Markus grumbled.

"Oh, oh! What's that? Red pepper flake. Hang on... Hang on... I swear I remember you saying your dad or someone owned a restaurant... No, it was your *uncle*, right? I'll bet you're there."

"I really think it's a bad idea for you to come over. It'd be a waste of your time! There's *no Structo*-whatever here. Just... give me a primer on what they eat and what to watch out f—"

"Here we go, Dimitrios's Bistro, Crested Butte, Colorado. I'll be there in seventeen minutes, according to Google. See you then."

Boop.

Markus looked at his phone as the screen winked off. He sighed. "Yeah, great. Let's do that. The more the merrier."

He pocketed the phone and turned to Blodgett. The creature had pushed open the door to the storeroom and snagged a cardboard box, fortunately without destroying another doorway. Box in tow, it lumbered into the center of the dining room and plopped down on the floor, knocking a few framed prints from the walls, and tore the top of the box open.

"Blodgett, listen, I don't know if you should be messing with the stuff you find in this place. Gale's coming over and she'll know what to do."

The creature stopped rummaging and looked at Markus while he was talking. Once he was through with the warning, Blodgett blinked once and cheerfully ignored it. The box was full of small tin cans with tomatoes on the label. In proportion to Blodgett, they looked like jelly beans, and the creature treated them in much the same way. Clapping its hand to its open mouth, it popped a half dozen of the cans inside.

"*Don't!*" Markus yelped.

Blodgett crunched down and munched happily on the chewy snack. Despite having chomped on something that would give a garbage disposal trouble, the mouthful seemed to go down just fine. After a satisfied gulp, the hungry creature wiped a smear of thick red paste away with the back of its hand and belched light-ly. The air filled with the aroma of roasted tomato.

"Okay… Okay, that's fine then. Keep doing that. At least that's only mildly destructive."

***

Twenty minutes, eighteen cans of tomato paste, three canisters of oregano, and six pounds of whole wheat flour later, Blodgett seemed satisfied. Now it was offering a handful of tins of ancho-vies to Markus.

"No, that's all right. Thanks," Markus said, waving off the "treat." "I filled up on assorted canned goods on the way over. I'm stuffed, honest."

Blodgett shrugged and popped one of the cans into its mouth. The can squished easily between its still-unseen teeth, but as soon as the juice hit Blodgett's tongue it became clear this was *not* as tasty as the last few snacks. A rusty red tongue dangled from its mouth and it spat the half-chewed can of fish to the floor, churring unhappily and lumbering to the mostly trashed back room to tug at the broken sprinkler.

"It'll eat raw flour, but even this thing won't eat anchovies. I'm starting to wonder why they even sell them," he muttered, making his way to the utility room to turn the water back on so the beast could rinse the taste out of its mouth.

The twisted pipe began to gush water, and Blodgett eagerly latched on, guzzling at the cool drink. After a minute or two, it turned aside, released a steamy sigh of relief, and wandered back into the dining room.

"If this is going to be a long-term thing, I'm going to have to teach you to turn off the water when you're done," he said, head-ing to the utility room.

He'd only just finished turning off the flow to the sprinklers when an overenthusiastic knock rattled the door.

"Mark! Mark, it's Gale! Lemme in! Come on!" called Gale from the other side of the door.

The sudden racket startled Blodgett. The creature jumped, shaking the whole building when it landed, then thundered back through the much-abused door to the place where the pizza oven had originally been. Once there, it crouched down and tucked its head and arms in as best it could, like a turtle trying to pull into its shell. Though it certainly looked more like a pizza oven now than when it was standing, the illusion wasn't exactly convincing, particularly with the metal plates rattling together as the creature trembled like a pup.

"Seriously, Blodgett?" Markus snickered.

He opened the door and was nearly trampled by an eager young woman with an armload of textbooks and notepads.

Gale was twenty-five years old and pleasantly plump, though with the energy of a caffeinated preschooler. Perhaps as a side effect of her intended career as a large-animal researcher, she tended to dress like a handler at a zoo, with khaki cargo shorts and a dark blue tee with a zebra-as-barcode logo on the front. Her youthful enthusiasm was underscored by a set of anachronistic braces and a pair of round-rimmed glasses that were almost comically oversized.

She slammed the door behind her. "Where is it? Where's the—jeez, this place is a mess."

"Yes, apparently that tends to happen when there's a giant animal loose in an eatery. It's in the back there, through the newly renovated doorway. You might have to look closely. It's a master of camouflage," he said flatly.

He took two steps forward to lead her there, but she blasted past him, fumbling for the camera slung around behind her. Behind him he heard another female voice, one that was withered yet piercing in a way that only an elderly woman can manage.

"Markus? Markus Spiros, is that you I hear down there?"

"Crap… That's Mrs. Penny, the lady upstairs. I'm surprised she hasn't called the cops already, with the racket I've been making. I've got to take care of this. Are you going to be okay in here?"

Rather than an answer, a series of camera flashes and exclamations of scientific excitement came from the back room.

"... Yeah, you'll be fine." He pulled open the door and stepped outside. "Mrs. Penny! I'm glad I caught you! I, uh... hope the construction isn't bothering you. Big problem with the plumbing, gotta gut the whole kitchen..."

***

He talked to Mrs. Penny for four or five minutes, which was probably the record for shortest conversation he'd ever had with her; but knowing Gale and Blodgett were together in the other room was a strong impetus to keep it short. While he was reasonably sure Blodgett wouldn't do anything unfortunate to the girl, he was less sure Gale would be able to restrain herself from terrorizing the poor thing with her boundless curiosity and zeal for investigation.

"Okay, hopefully we'll get this wrapped up quickly, Mrs. Penny. Thank you!" Markus said, slipping back in the door and locking it. "Boy," he said, turning away from the door, "I'm actually kind of proud of the story I came up... with."

Gale was standing directly in front of him, arms crossed and a look of righteous fury in her eyes. Despite being a full foot shorter than him, she managed to achieve a remarkable level of intimidation.

"What did you do to that poor creature?" she demanded viciously.

"Whoa, I didn't do anything, Gale. Honest!"

"Obviously! There are *clear* signs of neglect! No wonder you didn't want me to come over. Give me one good reason I shouldn't turn you in for animal cruelty!"

"Because until a few minutes before I called you, I hadn't set foot in this place in years!" he said. "Why, what's wrong?"

"What's wrong?! Look at it! It's terrified!"

Markus looked through the door to the kitchen. Sure enough, Blodgett was still rattling with anxiety. He walked up to the clattering mass.

"Blodgett? Buddy?" he offered.

Blodgett blinked its eyes open, then lunged forward to wrap Markus in a tight, hot, *relieved* hug.

"This does not strike me as the result of abuse," Markus wheezed as he tried to pull himself free.

The creature spied Gale and tensed a bit. It released Markus, spinning him around by the shoulders and huddling "behind" him as though Markus would protect it from Gale.

"I think it just doesn't like strangers. Blodgett and I... we've sort of got a history that I didn't know about."

Gale's expression eased, but only slightly. "Fine... but... get it out here into the light."

It took some coaxing by the hand, but Markus managed to lead the creature back into the dining room. On the way out it snagged the sooty old delivery jacket and clutched it like a security blanket.

"Look, you see this?" Gale said, indicating the crusty brown skin of Blodgett's arm. "It should look more like rising dough than a pretzel. This is a clear sign of overheating."

"Really?" Markus said, looking with concern at Blodgett. "Is it... is it bad? Is it going to be okay? Does it need treatment?"

"It isn't *good*," Gale said, dragging out a textbook and flipping through. "At *this* level, there should be only cosmetic damage. But a few more days and it could have been *far* worse. Your specimen here... *Blodgett*, is it? ... is in the early stages of its escalating exothermic transition. Until it develops heat vents, it's going to have to manually regulate its heat levels both internally and externally with water much more often than an adult. Ideally it would have a body of cool water to drink and soak in as needed."

"Right now we've just got the busted sprinkler system."

"It'll do in a pinch, but you'll need to improve that. What have you been feeding it?"

"Back when I thought it was just an oven, it was chunk charcoal. Since I found it this way, mostly whole canned goods and bags of flour. I can't imagine that's very healthy for it."

"Well, it's not ideal, but it's pretty close, actually." She leafed through the text. "At this stage, you'll want to wean off charcoal, which is basically baby food, and make the switch to kiln-dried hardwood and assorted unprocessed ores. Mostly... iron, zinc, tin, and copper. Plus, whatever dried herbs best suit its tastes. This oven is less than ideal. Solid metal is far too rigid for proper development, but *that* damage is done, unfortunately. Hence the squat build and crinkled neck and tail."

As Gale, now calmer, failed to maul the poor defenseless beast, Blodgett began to very slowly become more at ease. Still from the safety of its hiding place behind Markus, the creature crouched down and plucked up a can of anchovies, tossing them forward as a peace offering.

"Oh, thank you!" Gale said brightly, placing down her textbook to pick up the tin. "That's very generous."

"You actually like anchovies?" Markus said.

"Sure, they're great," she said, peeling back the lid to pluck out one of the salty fish and pop it into her mouth. "Usually I don't eat them straight, but I wouldn't want to appear ungrateful." She turned to Blodgett and rubbed her stomach theatrically. "Mmm. *Very good.*"

"You're weirder than I remember..."

"You know, you've got to find a home for this little lady."

"Little lady? It's a female?"

"Well, I mean, the sexual dimorphism in the *Structophis gastrignae* is virtually nonexistent. There's some evidence to suggest the species may be hermaphroditic at birth. But at full adulthood they often choose to present as male or female, at the very least. Studies have shown a correlation between certain behaviors and apparent genders." She held up the tin of anchovies. "*This* is one of them. Did it try to feed you?"

"Uh... Yeah, actually."

"Then best guess right now is we've got a *she*, not an it. At least until she tells us otherwise."

"Ah... So I guess I should be going with Blodg*ette* instead of Blodgett."

"Whatever you like. But like I was saying, you need to find a home for her."

"Yeah... I guess so. Who would I call to handle that? Do I hand her over to a preservation program or—"

"No, you don't understand. *You* need to find her a home. She's your responsibility now."

"Why me? I barely knew she existed until today."

"Because she's comfortable with you. Markus, this creature probably only fully emerged a few days ago. One of the most remarkable things about *Structophis gastrignae* is the true emergence period. Right now Blodgette is probably somewhere in the vicinity of a five-year-old human, mentally. By this time next year she'll be closer to a ten-year-old. And within two years she'll have caught up to *us* and stabilized there. Imagine collapsing your whole childhood into two years. This is a phenomenally important time in Blodgette's psychological development. And if you're already a trusted figure, then for the next two years, *you're* the papa."

"Whoa, hey. I'm not ready to be raising a two-thousand-pound daughter. Great Uncle Dimitrios has been taking care of her for the last few years. Surely *he'll* fit the daddy role."

"Sure, maybe. Where is he, anyway? He's got a lot to answer for."

"I don't know."

"Then that doesn't really help you much, does it? Plus, there's still the other issue."

"Which is?"

"That flakey golden crust and the stunted growth are still evidence of mishandling and mistreatment, even if she seems to be fairly healthy. We're talking about an endangered species, Mark. If the authorities see what she looks like before she's old enough to fend for herself, you're looking at jail time, and might I remind you that you being locked up means she won't get the proper care she needs."

"... This keeps getting better," Markus said, eyes wide and distant.

Blodgette, apparently feeling Markus needed some comforting, plopped her chin onto his shoulder, nearly knocking him over.

"Hey, look at the bright side," Gale said, raising the camera and snapping a picture.

"There's a bright side?"

"Sure." Gale admired the preview on the DSLR's screen. "Auntie Gale is going to have one hell of a great thesis when this is all over."

Chapter 3

Markus was swiftly learning a few things about being Blodgette's caretaker. She was very, *very* clingy, particularly with Gale about. Even after the overt terror of a hyperactive and critically fascinated aspiring large-animal veterinarian had faded, the dragon was still unwilling to leave Markus alone long enough to get anything done. She had one pudgy mitt wrapped around his. Her other hand held an old delivery boy jacket, and whenever Gale came close enough to touch her, Blodgette would huddle a little closer to Markus.

The endless sequence of Gale's investigations and Blodgette's retreats had pinned Markus into the corner of the dining room, trying to use his free hand to juggle both a stack of old-fashioned address books and his cell phone.

"Uh-huh. Yes. This is his nephew. Well, a few levels further removed than that but—no. ... No, I don't need more vinyl repair kits. The booth chairs are fine. I'm just wondering if maybe Dimitrios told you where he was going, because the business is sort of falling to pieces without him. ... Okay. Thanks for your help. Yes, I'll make sure I tell him hello when I find him."

Markus ended the call and tried to look past Blodgette, whose bulky form almost entirely filled his vision.

"Gale, are you still here?" he asked, standing on his tiptoes to look over Blodgette's shoulder.

The creature released a concerned warble and took a half step back, flattening Markus against the wall. A moment later there was the flash of a camera and the furious scratching of pen on paper.

"Yeah, you're still here. Could you move back a bit? I feel like a knickknack that slid down behind the armoire and was never heard from again."

She must have done so, because Markus could feel Blodgette become less tense. With a gentle nudge, which for a behemoth like Blodgette nearly needed to be delivered with a baseball bat, he coaxed her out of the way and led her to the center of the room.

"Well, that's it. He didn't cancel any deliveries, didn't reroute any mail, and he hasn't told anyone where he's going."

"Shouldn't you be worried?" Gale asked, snapping another picture as Blodgette shuffled behind Markus and plopped down.

"A normal person doing that would worry me, but Dimitrios is the guy who decided three days into his honeymoon that he wanted to find out what buffalo mozzarella tasted like, so he went to Germany for two weeks."

"...Why Germany?"

"He thought that's where buffalo mozzarella came from. How's Blodgette doing?"

"It's kind of hard to tell; she's really skittish. Traditionally, *Structophis gastrignae* are raised as sort of a community project. Everyone takes turns shoveling coal, and when the true emergence begins the whole town gathers to witness it. If you and your great uncle are the only ones who ever fed her, and she emerged alone or maybe with just Dimitrios to see it, she might take a while to adjust to new faces. But her health is very good, considering. Which reminds me. I found this in the kitchen. See if you can get her to open wide for me."

Gale held up a digital fry thermometer with a long probe.

"Why...?"

"Internal temperature is very important. We can't risk her getting overheated, it could be fatal. She's gone long enough since her last drink that she's probably at about equilibrium, so this will give us a good idea of where she is in her development."

Markus turned to the creature. She turned happily to him and grinned, an expression that was mostly visible in the angle of her mask and the sliver of lip exposed on either side.

"Okay, Blodgette. I need you to open your mouth."

Blodgette cocked her head to the side.

"She's smart, Markus, but she's not going to understand the whole language just yet. You're going to have to demonstrate," Gale said.

"Like this. *Ahhh.* See? Do this. *Ahhh*," he said, pointing eagerly at his mouth.

Blodgette squinted, then climbed to her feet and shuffled toward the kitchen, taking him by the hand and tugging him after her.

"Okay, what did I say? Where are we going?" Markus said.

She stopped at the doorway and merely reached inside, snagging a stick of pepperoni and turning to hand it to him.

"What? ... Oh. No, that wasn't a baby-bird 'feed me' ahh. That was a 'you do this' ahh."

He gestured with his hands and demonstrated repeatedly, Gale doing the same, until Blodgette finally followed suit.

"*Ahhhhhhhhh*," she said, that particular vocalization within her range.

The "voice," such as it was, certainly had a very distinctive quality. It was a bit like a parrot's imitation of speech, closer to a tweet that had been extended and smoothed out than something someone would confuse for a legitimate human. It was also several octaves deeper, putting one in mind of the sound a tugboat would make.

Far more distinctive, however, was the *breath*. It had all the same scents as a brick-oven pizzeria working at full bore: the tomatoes, seasonings, crust, and coal all contributing to a pleasant, rustic aroma. It was also incredibly hot, akin to the rush of hot air one gets when checking on a Thanksgiving turkey.

Gale placed the tip of the probe under Blodgette's tongue and watched the number start to tick up.

"See if you can get her to close her mouth but not bite down," Gale said.

Markus shrugged and mimed the required motion with both his mouth and his hand, closing each slowly until she began to imitate. When it was closed enough, he stopped and held up his hands. She stopped and held up hers as well.

"*Yeah!*" Markus crowed, high-fiving one of Blodgette's raised hands.

The creature looked curiously at him, then returned the gesture. With all her size and weight behind it, the blow knocked him to the ground. Blodgette's eyes shot open, and she chirped in dismay, crouching to pull him to his feet and wrapping him in an almost-but-not-quite-too-tight hug.

"It's okay, pal," he groaned. "No harm, no foul. ... Please let go. I have to breathe."

While the dragon reluctantly loosened her grip on Markus, Gale took the thermometer from where it had fallen and checked the peak value.

"Yeah... We're up near eight hundred degrees. I'd say we've got about three days before a spritz with a sprinkler isn't going to cut it anymore. We've got to get Blodgette someplace better suited to her needs, and we've got to start her on better eating habits. Decent hardwood, good ores. If she gets onto good nutrition now, over the course of her growth, she'll incorporate all of this into her body and hopefully grow beyond it. She'll be smaller than she should be, but she can still recover a bit."

Markus blew an exasperated breath and stepped back from the clingy creature.

"Okay, okay. Let me think. Water and wood are easy enough to get. Ore is the tricky one. Where do you get ore?"

"Quarries," Gale said absently, digging through her bag.

"Well yeah, but you don't just sign up and take a crate of unprocessed iron."

"She won't need much. It isn't as if she digests it; it just works its way into her body where she needs it and stays there. Stuff they discard from commercial quarries is more than rich enough."

"So an exhausted quarry would work? Because my Aunt Beeni used to take us to this quarry lake when I was little. There was a campground. Should be pretty easy to get wood. I forget why we stopped going."

Gale found what she was looking for. It was one of those bizarre infrared thermometers with the laser dot that looked as if it should be used to maintain equipment on the USS *Enterprise*. While Markus started to dial his aunt, she angled it at Blodgette, who eyed it with a suitable level of distrust.

"Get her to lift her arm. I want to see what the surface temperature is in the armpit."

"Blodgette, look at me. Go like this now," Markus whispered, briefly holding the phone away from his ear and angling his arm out.

Blodgette swung her arm out. She knocked over a chair but didn't pay any mind to that or the strange woman pointing a bizarre device at her armpit. All she seemed to care about was matching his position and watching him for approval.

"Okay, got it," Gale said, checking the readout and marking it down.

"Good job!" Markus whispered, holding his hand out for a high five again.

She reared back for a good hard slap.

"No, no, no!" Markus said with a cringe.

Blodgette froze for a moment, then looked at her hand and, with a wave of understanding, delivered a light pat rather than a devastating blow.

"*Good job!*" Markus said again. "Oh! Uh, no, I wasn't talking to you, Aunt Beeni. … Yes, I'm taking care of things at the bistro. No, I haven't heard from Uncle Dimitrios. … Yes, I remember him…"

***

A rather ragged and frayed rental car rattled its way down a narrow street, and out from inside stumbled an equally ragged and frayed man. He was spry for his age, which was probably into his eighties, but had made the distinctive fashion choices of a man who either didn't know or didn't care how ridiculous he looked. He was wearing a pair of sunglasses still sporting the price tag. They had the sleek design and accent of glitter that suggested he may have selected a woman's design, but that fact didn't faze him in the slightest. They actually went rather well with his similarly fresh-from-the-store shorts and shirt, each with a flamboyant design. The overall look was that of a man who was either trying to blend in and failing miserably or attempting to stand out and succeeding brilliantly.

He brushed his fingers through an unkempt mane of white hair and slid his sunglasses down his short, stubby nose to peer over them. This revealed a set of eyebrows thick enough to lose a comb in and a pair of mischievous brown eyes. Satisfied with whatever he'd been looking for, he restored the glasses and grinned. He had a bushy beard and mustache, as unruly as the rest of the hair on his head, and his teeth had the pristine whiteness and unnatural straightness of a well-made set of dentures.

After patting every individual pocket of his outfit twice, he revealed an ancient billfold and flipped it open. The inside was stuffed to bursting with everything but money. There were receipts, coupons, hotel keys, ticket stubs, and a thick stack of business cards. From behind a badly expired Colorado driver's license issued to "Dimitrios A. Spiros" he pulled a worn card.

"Seven-four-four Sorrento..." he muttered, raising an eyebrow and glancing at the nearest doors.

The street had seen better days. Once part of a thriving downtown, now most of the shops were vacant, condemned, or on their way to such a fate. The address he was after was only a short walk away. It was a good solid door, faded paint suggesting a formerly elegant appearance that now underscored its lack of upkeep. Grime-encrusted windows revealed mostly emptied shelves. A few lingering knickknacks and curiosities suggested the store had once been a treasure trove of antiques.

"I could swear this place was a tourist hot spot last time I was here. Leave a place for a decade and look what happens," Dimitrios said.

He pushed his sunglasses down again and fumbled in his pocket for a prepaid flip-style cell phone. Tapping out the number on the business card earned him little more than a voice informing him in Italian that the number was no longer in service.

"Now that's some fine customer service. No wonder they went out of business, not offering support for their products. Oh... What's this?"

Dimitrios leaned low and brushed the curled edge of an old flyer that had been pasted on the door. It was nearly as faded as the paint, but the message was still readable.

"'This property has been acquired by Hearst LTD,'" he read aloud. "'Direct all inquiries to our home offices.' Now we're getting somewhere."

He punched the provided number into his phone. It barely had a chance to ring before it was answered by a man with crisp German diction.

Halfway through the greeting, Dimitrios stopped him. "That's enough of that. If we're going to be doing business, we'll be doing it in English, thank you very much."

"Ah. My apologies," the man said.

It is said that Germans are extremely efficient, and there must be some truth to that, because he managed to communicate his instant and undying disdain for Dimitrios utilizing nothing more than the tone of his otherwise mannerly reply.

"You have reached Hearst Limited. My name is Hans. How may I be of help to you?" said Hans.

"I'm standing here in front of Carlos's Antiques in Naples, Italy, and I've got some care-and-feeding questions for something I purchased a few years back."

"One moment, sir... Would that be Antiquariato di Carlo?"

"I suppose."

"Yes, I see that the establishment was indeed added to our holdings some time ago. I'm afraid... one moment..." Hans's voice became a degree more serious. "What precisely is the product you require help with today, sir?"

"That's between me and Carlos."

"The former proprietor's name was Carlo, not Carlos, and I am afraid I cannot help you with your purchase if you will not offer at least a description."

"Let's just say it was an investment. It has matured. I had this big book he gave me with instructions on how to... maintain the investment after maturity. But it got set on fire. So I need to know the short version of how to keep this thing fed and watered and such."

"So you purchased a *creature* from this shop."

"I never said that."

"Then why do you require instruction regarding food?"

"Look, the damn thing is walking around now, and I just need some rules."

"Hold please, sir."

A few clicks and secondary dials, and a short period of listening to German hold music ended with a new voice on the phone.

"Hello, sir," said the new man.

His voice was quite different. There was no trace of an accent. Not German, not English, not any flavor of American. It was the most sterile, clinical phrasing Dimitrios had ever heard, as if the person had learned the language by simply uploading the dictionary into his brain.

"Are you the man who can tell me about how to care for my investment?" Dimitrios asked.

"That would depend upon how you answer the next question. The item you purchased. Was it a small lump of oddly rounded charcoal?"

"That's what it *looked* like, sure. It hasn't looked that way in a while. Now that it's up and about, I've got to get the thing figured out before it goes belly up."

"I see. I'm going to ask you to go to my local offices. Hans will have a car sent for you, if you like. I'll be stepping on my personal jet directly. I'll be there in three hours. You and I have some matters to discuss in person. Until I arrive, I will leave instructions for my people to provide you with whatever it is you might require. We have much to discuss."

"Now *that's* more like it. I'll make sure Carlos knows you're doing a good job for him."

"Thank you, sir. I look forward to our meeting."

Dimitrios nodded, not seeming to mind that such a gesture wasn't terribly useful in a telephone conversation, then hung up. He pocketed the phone and rubbed his hands together enthusiastically.

"This is it, Dimitrios. Your ship is finally coming in. That thing is going to be a gold mine…"

Chapter 4

"Okay. ... Okay, Aunt Beeni. Thanks. Yes. ... No. ... I—... You said that already. ... I've... *I've got to go, Aunt Beeni.* Love you too. Bye."

Markus hastily hung up the phone before his aunt could work her way through another cycle of irrelevant anecdotes. Blodgette chirruped happily at the sight of the phone being tucked away again.

"Sorry for the wait, buddy," he said, offering a pat on the head as consolation.

"Find anything out?" Gale asked, underlining some of her notes and then fetching a tape measure from her things.

"That quarry lake is a nature reserve. No more camping or swimming there. She says the state barely even patrols it anymore and that's a 'darn shame.'"

"Well that's some good news. Blodgette is nature, and she needs preserving, so that lake is just the thing."

"Yeah, assuming we can get her there. How about you, find anything out?"

"The vital statistics are all on the low end of acceptable. I'd like to get some X-rays of her neck and tail to make sure they're not too bad. But the most fascinating stuff is the social aspect. You're sure you never worked with her at all post-emergence?"

"I haven't been back here since the day she crawled at me. It seriously weirded me out."

"So she was barely into the ambulatory phase when you checked out, and yet she fully recognizes and trusts you specifically, but not me. As far as I know, Blodgette is the first recorded case of a *Structophis gastrignae* raised in such an isolated way. Neither her parents nor a human family or community. *Structophis gastrignae* as a species have always been known to be very social, but we've never known the degree of recognition present in early development. This is... groundbreaking! I'd love to see how she reacts to Dimitrios. Does she feel more strongly about him than you? What's the more vital period of emotional connection?"

"Yeah," he groaned. "I'd like to know how she feels about Uncle Dimitrios too. Because that'd mean we'd have *found* Uncle Dimitrios, and thus this would be at least partially *his* problem to help solve. But Uncle Dimitrios is busy being Uncle Dimitrios."

"Boy, that name's a mouthful. Don't you have a nickname or anything for him?"

"This coming from the girl who insists on calling Blodgette a *Structophis gastrignae*."

"What would you prefer?"

"Pizza dragon. The common name for them."

"That's an oversimplification."

"Yes, Gale, that's what nicknames are."

"Fine. You can call her that if you want, but I'm sticking with *Structophis gastrignae*."

Markus looked wearily to Blodgette, who once again offered a subtle grin and clutched his hand in her mitt.

"Okay, Gale. Give me the run down. What's it take to keep Blodgette happy and healthy?"

"Companionship plus social and intellectual enrichment will be key for her happiness. Talk to her a lot. Ask her questions, play games. We've been through the food. Make plenty of firewood and ore available to her. She'll eat what she needs. Lots of ingredients too. Herbs and spices, flour, things like that. That should keep her healthy. Later she'll develop other interests and compulsions, but those are for her to discover, not you."

He nodded distantly. Blodgette mimicked him and then raised her hand for a high five, which he offered with a smirk. The positive expression didn't last long. Blodgette squinted at him and warbled something low. Even without words, it seemed like a sound of concern.

"Remarkable emotional empathy even so near to emergence," Gale observed, scratching another note into her pad. "What's wrong?"

"I had a midterm coming up. Not going to be able to do that. I've got work tomorrow. That's not going to happen. This is a huge monkey wrench in my life. I'm not sure how I'm going to make it work." He sighed. "Thanks for helping out, though. I guess you can get going. I'll call you if I have more questions. At least until they turn my phone off."

"Nope."

"Nope what?"

"I'm not going anywhere. This is my thesis now, buster. I'm a grad student. My room and board is paid for, so long as I'm working on course credits, and this here could keep me in research straight through to my doctorate if I play my cards right. Plus, all things considered she's a bit of a problem child. So for her sake and yours, I wouldn't want you fumbling around without my advice."

"Really?"

"Yep. And right now, my advice is to get this young lady to that lake where she'll be able to take better care of herself. How are we going to do that?"

"Uh…" He looked around and spied the keys on the hook beside the cash register. "Let me have that measuring tape. I've got to go measure the catering truck. We might be able to load her in there."

Gale tossed the tape. Markus caught it and headed for the back door. He made it all of three steps before Blodgette realized he was going somewhere and grabbed him by the arm, hauling him into a clingy hug and churring worriedly.

"Okay," he wheezed, waggling the tape measure in his hand since his arms were clamped to his sides. "You go measure."

"Hang on," she said, pulling up her camera and flipping it on. "This is a behavior worth documenting."

"You're sure this isn't just because I look ridiculous," he croaked as Blodgette swung her crinkled tail around in front of her and wrapped it around his legs in a sort of secondary hug.

"You don't look ridiculous, you look adorable."

She snapped a picture. The flash spooked Blodgette slightly, causing her to hug a bit tighter and watch Gale with suspicion until the girl took the tape measure and left the room.

"You know, at some point you're going to have to let me go," Markus said.

Blodgette churred happily, the deep sound reverberating all through her body, vibrating her hard enough to cause some of the smaller metal plates of her armor to jingle. She rocked side to side a bit, then traded the hug for a firm grip around his wrist again as she led him around the dining room, pointing her stubby fingers at some of the pictures on the walls.

This being a family establishment, it would have made sense if the pictures had been pictures of Dimitrios himself or maybe of his nieces and nephews. (He never had any children of his own.) Instead the pictures were primarily of other business ventures Dimitrios had embarked on. The bistro was his second major business, and so far the only one to have any degree of success. The two major endeavors joined possibly hundreds of lesser ventures that had ended catastrophically.

Blodgette pulled a framed photo of a goat ranch off the wall.

"Yeah, that's Dimitrios's ranch back in Greece. Goat's milk and olives were what he was selling. Then for some reason he tried to switch over to camel milk. Didn't work out."

Blodgette dropped the picture absentmindedly, stepping back startled when it shattered on the floor.

"Maybe let's not drop these," he said, picking it up and placing it on a table.

She selected another picture from the wall.

"I think this was when he decided it would be a good idea to make cars that ran on yeast or something. Not only did they not work, but they were incredibly ugly. I think this was one of those situations when Uncle Dimitrios assumed he could do something simply because he didn't understand why he couldn't."

They worked their way through the rest of the pictures on the wall, which formed a conga line of half-baked and quarter-baked ideas. One was an attempt to combine bungee jumping and high diving. Another was a hot-air balloon service that attempted to serve hotdogs cooked on the balloon's burner. His uncle was without a doubt a visionary. Unfortunately, he was a visionary in the same way that a frequent peyote user was a visionary.

"And this is a picture of Dimitrios investing in a distillery to make fifty-year brandy. I guess the first barrels of that are going to be showing up in another ten years," Markus said, setting down the final picture. "Say what you will about my great uncle, the man didn't blow all his money on get-rich-quick schemes. He was more than willing to get rich slow."

He frowned as a thought came to mind. "Now that I think about it, you're pretty much definitely part of one of those schemes. And I can't think of a single use he might have in mind for you that wouldn't severely sour my opinion of him..."

Gale stepped inside, dusting off her hands. Blodgette gave her a suspicious look and grabbed Markus's arm.

"Okay, I measured the inside, I looked up the route to that quarry lake of yours, and I did the math. There's *just* enough room for us to load you, Blodgette, and enough containers of water to keep her below critical temperature for the ride, assuming we are able to stop at least twice to top off the water."

"Room for *me* in the back. But... Yeah... I guess she's not going to let me out of her sight for a five-hour road trip."

"I'm betting she's not going to be fond of letting you out of her sight for long enough to take a bathroom break, even. So if I was you, I'd take care of that before we leave."

"That catering truck isn't automatic, you know. Do you know how to drive a stick?"

"Markus, I've got ninety-four college credits. I think I can probably handle driving a truck with three pedals instead of two. Now come on. Time's a-wasting and it looks as if there're a bunch of shelves and stuff to clear out of the back before we can fit the two of you back there. Let's get cracking!"

"Oh," he said, reaching into his pocket. "Speaking of cracking, do me a favor and hold my phone. Something tells me Blodgette's affection's as likely as not to break it before I can get her to figure out how fragile the world is compared to her."

He handed it to her. She slipped it into her pocket.

"Everything will be just fine now that I'm helping plan this operation," Gale said.

***

Several hours later, in Italy, Dimitrios Spiros sat in a strangely sterile waiting room. He'd done business with plenty of wealthy men and women in the past. *Usually* they liked to fill the areas where they would entertain clients and the like with things that would leave an impression of wealth and competence. Custom commissioned works of art from respected artists were common, or even masterpieces from the handful of painters whom the general public actually knew by name.

This place was considerably different. The walls were stark white and decorated with black-and-white photographs hung in black frames, each depicting mundane objects like ancient rotary phones or large rusty keys. The furniture was all matte black and perfectly angular: rectangular chairs with square cushions, oddly tall, spindly tables. It felt like the sort of room someone would put together to perform a dubiously ethical psychological experiment. Or it would have to anyone but Dimitrios. He took the room in, ran it through his brain for a few moments, and assigned it the label "modern."

He was leafing through an architecture portfolio he'd found on the table when the door opened. The man who entered practically embodied the word "corporate." He was dressed impeccably in a black suit that anyone could agree was worth fifteen thousand dollars, though few would be able to explain *why*. The man was dark skinned, with a strong, square jaw that could well have served as inspiration for the room itself. His expression was even and dispassionate, though his eyes had the sharpness and focus of a man just as comfortable ordering an assassination as a martini. This, too, was lost on Dimitrios, who gave the man the same amount of thought as the room and arrived at the label "management."

"Dimitrios Aristotle Spiros?" asked the man.

Dimitrios stood, offering a hand. "That's me. Quite a place you've got here. You run it?"

"That I do, sir. Donald Hearst. Hearst Limited."

"Fine, fine. Very modern. You know I'm an entrepreneur as well."

"So I've seen. I took the time during my flight to familiarize myself with your investment history. It has been quite diverse."

"Never good to put all your eggs in one basket. And nothing ventured nothing gained."

"Words to live by. Though it should be said that a bit more care could be taken as to which baskets you've chosen to store your eggs, as merely venturing is not nearly sufficient to guarantee gains."

Spiros nodded, though his expression suggested he'd stopped listening after "words to live by." "So, about that customer support question I had."

"Yes, I would very much like to address that. Please, take a seat," Hearst said.

Dimitrios did so. Hearst sat opposite him.

"Now, regarding these ventures of yours. One of them is Dimitrios's Bistro, correct?"

"Yes."

"And you've only got a single location in Colorado?" he asked.

"I was waiting to solidify my business plan before franchising," Dimitrios said.

"Established 1964. A half century has not been sufficient to suitably solidify your business plan?"

"Better safe than sorry."

"Again, words to live by. Your knowledge of platitudes is encyclopedic, sir."

"Why all the interest in my dining establishment?"

"I just needed to confirm ownership. One moment," Hearst said.

He removed a sleek smartphone from his pocket and tapped the screen.

"I've indeed confirmed the Colorado location," he said. "I hope you don't mind, Mr. Spiros…"

"Call me Dimitrios, please."

"Dimitrios, I've got a rather large staff supporting me at all times, and rather than take them away from their equipment and resources, I've left them at the home office. To keep them apprised of the content of this conversation, I'd like your permission to put the rest of it on speakerphone."

"If that's how you do business, I wouldn't want to interrupt."

"A sensible man," Hearst said, setting the phone down on the table. "There are a few more things I'd like to confirm before we address your 'customer support' issue. The item in question, you purchased it from an antiquities shop sometime between eight and thirteen years ago, correct?"

"That's right."

"And in the time since your acquisition, the item has been stored at a more or less constant temperature between eight hundred and a thousand degrees Fahrenheit?"

"Well, we didn't stick a thermometer in there, but roundabout there, yes."

"Good. And have you shared the location and nature of this item with anyone in any official capacity since its acquisition?"

"It isn't the sort of thing you spread around, Mr. Hearst."

Hearst grinned. "No, it isn't. And I am pleased to know you are intelligent enough to be mindful of that. Based upon the information provided, is it safe to assume that you've been keeping the item at the aforementioned bistro?"

"Yes. I've got to say, this is an awfully long customer survey before we get to my issue."

"It was necessary. I don't take action until I am certain it is warranted. Martinez, you may have the men move in," he said, addressing the phone with his final statement.

"Move in?" Dimitrios said.

"Well, Dimitrios. You and I are quite aware of the specifics, as is my staff. I believe we can safely discontinue the circumlocution and establish the proper context for future discussions. Fifteen years ago, a theft was reported at the Abbatia Territorialis Sanctae Mariae Montis Oliveti Maioris, an abbey that, for reasons beyond the scope of this conversation, was housing a clutch of seven eggs of an exotic species. For two years local and national authorities had sought the eggs. Eight years ago a trail of clandestine purchases and exchanges led the investigation to Antiquariato di Carlo. A raid was able to recover four of the eggs. Three had been sold previously. Owing to the extreme illegality of trafficking such items, Carlo kept no records, and thus the location of the remaining eggs could not be determined. It was then that I initiated my own investigation. In short order, two more eggs were revealed, but improper storage had rendered them nonviable."

Dimitrios shifted uncomfortably in his seat. "This isn't a bust, is it?"

"No, sir. Quite the opposite. I do not represent the authorities. I am an interested party. For nearly twenty years I've been attempting to acquire a *Structophis gastrignae*, for reasons not relevant at this time. They are very tightly controlled, illegal for personal ownership, and cleared only for *behavioral* research. I was beginning to believe even my own considerable resources would not enable me to acquire one. Now it would appear that not only have I found one, but it has already hatched."

"Ahem," Dimitrios said, crossing his arms. "That's *my* dragon you're talking about."

"We shall see... Martinez?" Hearst said.

"I'm getting a report from the field operatives now... there is no S.G. present at the location. Considerable evidence of recent damage, but no staff or personnel present. Interview with the upstairs resident of the property suggests a young man and woman recently departed in a large vehicle. The S.G. may have been transported from the premises."

Hearst raised his eyebrow. "I may have underestimated you, Dimitrios. It takes a special man to get a step ahead of me."

"Yes... Yes, you've got to get up pretty early to catch Dimitrios sleeping..."

"You had no idea the creature wouldn't be there, did you?" Hearst said.

"Of course I did! I arranged the whole thing!" Dimitrios said. "And let me tell you this, *Mr. Hearst*. If you think you're going to turn me in for having that thing, I promise you you'll never find it. I'd rather see it turned in to... whoever takes those things from people who aren't supposed to have them than see another business profit from my legwork!"

Hearst looked at him doubtfully. He glanced at the phone. "Martinez, do we have an ID on the likely transporters?"

"The man was identified as Markus Spiros. No word yet on the woman."

"Get some men on Markus. Find out where he was, where he might have gone, et cetera."

"Already on it."

"Good." Hearst looked to Dimitrios. "Now, sir. I can see you are a patient man, and recent evidence suggests you are a stubborn one. As time is money, that has the potential to make you a *very* expensive man. Fortunately for you, I understand the value of a dollar, and I'm more than willing to part with it to get what I want. What is the asking price for the *Structophis gastrignae*?"

"Bah! It isn't *livestock*. I wasn't raising it to sell it. I had *plans* for that creature. Serious, ongoing plans."

"I see. And what were those plans?"

"And let you steal the idea? I'm not that foolish."

"Evidence suggests the contrary. Dimitrios, I have no interest in stealing your idea. You'll recall, I'm making a rather well-coordinated attempt to steal the *creature*. This discussion is occurring simply because there is the slim but real possibility that your obstinacy could keep me from my prize long enough for the authorities to intercept it or for the beast to be killed. If you've ever hoped to make a dime off the *Structophis gastrignae*, it would behoove you to talk business with me here and now. You won't have another opportunity."

"... Fine. It was going to be the mascot for the pizza delivery wing of the bistro franchise."

"... Mascot."

"Sure! A real live pizza dragon, helping to sell pizza? People would come from miles around to see it. The thing would be a national phenomenon. Not only would I push more product, I'd be able to sell merchandise! Hats, T-shirts, mugs, the works! It worked for Domino's with the Noid."

"Setting aside the dubious claim of success regarding a forgettable corporate icon of a bygone age, how precisely would you hope to publicly profit from the ownership of a creature that is illegal to own or acquire? The moment you revealed the *Structophis gastrignae*, at least three state and national agencies would demand you be placed behind bars."

"... I'd... I assumed I would figure that part out afterward. There's no problem too big that a little ingenuity can't solve it."

Hearst took a slow breath. "Very well. A moderately successful national campaign, beginning with a single location. Assuming a well-developed franchising plan initiated simultaneously, one can comfortably imagine two hundred national locations inside of five years. Extrapolating from your current location's revenue, projecting the revenue increase post-campaign, and integrating merchandise sales over that five-year period gives us what, Elizabeth?"

"One moment, sir..." said a voice over the phone.

"You are wasting your time, Hearst. I am a man of principle. I cannot be bought," Dimitrios said.

"Post-tax net income estimates fall between eight and fifteen million dollars, Mr. Hearst."

"Utterly incorruptible and—" Dimitrios continued.

"I'll give you thirty million dollars for the *Structophis gastrignae*."

"Sold," Dimitrios said. "What do you need me to do?"

"Right now, nothing. My accountant shall wire the first half of the payment to your account, following the application of your signature on the appropriate paperwork. Said paperwork will require you to provide any available and pertinent information required to locate and transfer ownership of the *Structophis gastrignae*."

"Mmm, yes. Fine, fine. But I'll be getting fifteen million up front and the rest after you get the thing, right?"

"Yes."

"Great. Good. Let's do that."

"Once again, I admire your principle, sir."

Blodgette illustrated by Cryptidshadows

Chapter 5

"Gale," Markus wheezed. "Are we there yet?"

"We'll get there when we get there," Gale grumbled from the driver's seat.

The trio had been on the road for a few hours, and as road trips go, Markus had been on better ones. When he had been six they'd taken a family road trip to the Grand Canyon, for example. On that trip he'd gotten food poisoning from a bad waffle, stepped in a pile of donkey flop, and gotten a terrible sunburn. That had been *vastly* superior to this journey because, while miserable, he had not been in mortal danger the whole time. At this moment, two things were competing for the honor of being the most bizarre cause of death to be recorded in a Colorado obituary. The first, and odds-on favorite, was Gale's driving.

A catering van is an unwieldy vehicle for the most experienced of drivers. A catering van loaded up with several hundred pounds of skittish pizza dragon is a good deal more difficult to handle. Gale was not only an inexperienced driver, she'd never even driven a manual transmission. The result was a swaying, veering, swerving journey punctuated with worrisome grinds, jerky acceleration, and assorted colorful phrases assigning blame to the other drivers. That they hadn't been pulled over for reckless driving was nothing short of a miracle.

All of this jarring motion had a fairly deleterious effect on the mental well-being of their primary passenger. Blodgette, who took up *most* of the available space in the hastily cleared rear portion of the van, had been in a state of wide-eyed panic for the duration of the drive. Markus had thus been called into service as her security blanket/teddy bear. She hugged him tightly against her in an embrace that made breathing a nontrivial endeavor. Every sudden jolt brought an additional squeeze and a warble of dismay. Her skin was very hot, and the metal of her pizza-oven-turned-suit-of-armor was only a few degrees short of sizzling.

They made a turn sharp enough for Blodgette to stumble aside, which almost certainly caused the whole vehicle to pitch onto two wheels.

"Is there time for me to dictate my will?" he said.

"Stop being so dramatic. We'll be there in an hour or so."

A smash outside caused Blodgette to release a startled peep that was downright adorable.

"What did we just hit?" Markus croaked.

"A mailbox."

"A private one or one of the big blue ones?"

"Does it matter?"

"I just want to know if it was a state or federal crime."

"Ha ha."

"Sarcastic laughter is only appropriate"—Blodgette clutched him a little tighter, reducing comment to a strangled wheeze again—"when I'm joking."

"How's Blodgette doing back there?"

"I'd say she's about eighty percent of the way to a full-blown phobia of driving, and with good reason."

"I mean *temperature* wise."

"Feeling a little toastier than usual, but she's not fidgeting or reaching for one of the bottles."

"And how are we set for water?"

They'd learned early on in the trip that the five-gallon water bottles they'd brought along for keeping Blodgette's temperature down needed to be *very* securely strapped to the walls of the van lest Gale's distinctive driving habits turn them into ballistic projectiles to batter and club Blodgette and Markus along the way. He swept his eyes across them. Most were empty now.

"Looks as if we've got one left, and it's only about half-full."

"Okay, it looks as if we're heading for some mountain roads. From the map, I'd say this is our last chance at civilization before we hit the quarry. I'm going to stop so we can top off the water and maybe grab some snacks."

She took another sharp turn to enter a parking lot. The way the whole van lurched upward and practically bashed Blodgette and Markus against the ceiling suggested she either accidentally or purposely jumped the curb rather than using that pesky driveway. After an attempted three-point turn ended up closer to a twenty-five-point turn, she hopped out of the driver's seat and pulled open the doors.

"Okay, everybody. Time to stretch our legs and get some fresh air."

Blodgette didn't need to be told to step out of the truck. The instant she saw daylight her eyes widened and she bolted for the doorway. The sudden motion of a massive beast making a desperate bid for the relative safety of the outside world caused the whole van to slide forward a few inches. She knocked Gale out of the way and thumped down onto the pavement, Markus still dangling from her embrace. Once she was on solid ground, she trembled lightly in both relief and the lingering stress of the many hours of hazardous journey so far.

"Oof. Both of you look like you could use a break," Gale said.

It was an understatement. Markus looked as if he'd been in a wrestling match with a bear. His hair and clothes were in utter disarray. Pure exhaustion showed in his expression, and every inch of his outfit was drenched with sweat from being wrapped in the doughy, crusty arms of an increasingly warm creature. Blodgette's expression, which came through surprisingly well considering the steel "mask" that covered most of her face, was rattled and ragged.

Markus looked at her wearily. "Tell me the truth, Gale. Have you ever driven before?"

"Hey, I just drove stick for the first time in my life, and it was for four straight hours with a squirmy, unrestrained load. I think I did pretty good. I didn't even get pulled over."

He glanced at the van. "There's a yield sign hooked on the rear bumper," he said.

"Ah…" She shrugged. "Well, still pretty good. Let's take a look at you, Blodgette."

Gale kicked the offending sign off the bumper and climbed into the back to fetch her tools of the trade. She had pulled the catering truck into the parking lot of what probably counted as the city center of this little mountain town. The standard small-town triumvirate of a barbershop, a café, and a post office stood across the street, along with a hardware store, a big box store, and assorted other mom-and-pop shops. The parking lot they'd stopped in wrapped around a fairly well-equipped garage and gas station. A pine forest grew steadily thicker behind the garage, climbing the slope up the frosty mountain beyond. Gale had strategically positioned the van such that Blodgette's hasty escape left her between the windowless rear of the garage and the forest, hidden from the road and all but the most dedicated busybodies.

The pizza dragon, now that the trauma of the rocky ride had begun to lose its edge, was realizing, for the first time, that she was *outdoors*. Not just outside the back room where she'd spent the first decade of her existence. Not just getting a glimpse of the sky out the window or while being coaxed into the truck. She was really and truly *outside*. Her luminescent eyes widened and she raised her head in wonder, gazing up at the piercing blue of the cloudless sky. She took a deep breath and released it in a scalding-hot sigh of contentment, then released Markus from the hug and instead grabbed his wrist to toddle along toward the trees. She burbled and warbled quietly, happiness and fascination evident even without language.

"Hey, let's not go too far," Markus said, casting nervous glances about. "We've come an awful long way without you getting noticed. I don't want to push my luck any further than I have to."

Blodgette crouched down and delicately plucked a wildflower from the ground. She held it up and turned it about, marveling at its color.

"Yeah. That's a flower. Give it a sniff," he said.

She chirruped and furrowed her brow.

"Like this, sniff," he said, leaning in to take a whiff.

Blodgette did the same, then chirped again more loudly and thudded off toward another cluster of flowers, dragging Markus along behind her.

"Hey! What did I say about not going too far!" he scolded.

She slowed down but didn't stop, looking him in the eye and slowly shuffling along as though if she did it slowly enough, it wouldn't count.

"Temperature check!" Gale said, marching up with her temp-gun and thermometer.

Though this was the first time they'd actually gotten out to do it, Gale had taken great care to have Blodgette's internal and external temperature measured at regular intervals. By now, Blodgette knew the drill and went through the motions while keeping her attention roughly on the cluster of flowers. She raised her arm, and Gale got a reading, then gave a good hearty "aaaah" for Gale to stick the thermometer in her mouth.

"Good job, buddy. You're getting good at that," Markus said, raising his hand for a high five.

To this Blodgette was willing to give her full attention. She gave his hand a good firm slap and peeped gleefully. She then started pulling flowers up by the handful. Big clumps of dirt hung from the roots as she held them to her snout to breathe in the scent. Once she'd sampled a bunch, she'd hand them to Markus and pick a new group to investigate.

"This is... odd..." Gale said, glancing over her notes.

"Yes, thank you, Blodgette," Markus said, accepting a third mound of flowers. "Odd good or odd bad?"

"Remains to be seen... but all the data *I've* seen suggests a *Structophis gastrignae* at her stage of development should be eagerly seeking quenching at about nine hundred degrees

Fahrenheit internal. Blodgette's up over nine hundred fifty and seems happy as a clam. No discomfort, no active searching for water. That's *well* outside the typical range."

"Oh man... I knew it. We screwed her up, right? She's sick. Body temperature running too high? That's a fever," he said, anxiety fluttering in his voice. "She's gonna die and I'm gonna go to jail..."

"In most creatures, sure. But the *Structophis gastrignae* isn't even close to being like most creatures. They're so variable in their physiology that all we can really work from is rules of thumb."

She pointed the temp-gun at Blodgette and took some surface measurements. "Her skin's right where it should be. Hence you not having first-degree burns from her hugs." She scratched her head. "Evidently Blodgette here is tolerant of much-higher temps than most at this stage of development. But there's still the question of where the heat's *going*. She's far too young to have developed heat vents for self-regulation..."

"Can we maybe look into this when we're somewhere that a cop probably won't wander over and ask me a bunch of uncomfortable questions?"

"Right, yeah. I'm going to take the van and fill her up. I see a deli. Do you want a sandwich or something?"

"No, please, don't waste any time. Just hurry up."

"Bah. You've got to eat something. I'll get you a sandwich while they're filling the truck." She started unloading the water jugs. "I see a hose over there. You fill these up while I'm out and about. And don't get into trouble."

"Okay, good, just *please* hurry!"

She hopped into the driver's seat. "I'll be back before you know it."

Illustrating the sort of driving skill that had made the trip thus far such an adventure, Gale managed to produce an echoing grind before finally getting the van in motion.

He shook his head and started to gather up the water jugs, muttering to himself. "You know, a *little* bit of anxiety would not be out of place, Gale," he said. "We *are* in the midst of... *some* kind of crime... There's probably a name for it. Owning an endangered species."

Markus realized half of his difficulty was that he was still holding the flowers Blodgette had given him, so he set them down and finally wrangled the jugs over to the water faucet. It was too much to hope for that the spigot be on the *back* of the building where he could fill it without fear of being seen. It was right on the side, where he had to stand more or less in direct view of the street.

"Okay, Blodgette, listen. ... Blodgette... *Blodgette!*"

The distracted dragon finally realized she was being beckoned and turned to thump over to him. Every step rattled the ground, and it was clear she wasn't terribly concerned about staying out of view.

"No, no, no!" he said, raising his hands. "You stay right there! Just, don't come over here."

Again she furrowed her brow, confused. She took another step.

"No! Down! Sit down. Look, see? Like this!"

He hastily demonstrated, taking a quick seat on the ground. She scratched her head. Then the realization dawned. She raised her tail a bit and flopped down onto the ground.

She'd not yet mastered the nuances of subtly, and thus her heavy flop felt as if someone had dropped a ton of bricks. It shook some needles from the nearby trees, and only through sheer luck did it fail to break the nearest window of the garage.

"Hey! What's going on back there?!" called a voice from the main building.

An elderly woman in a flannel shirt and overalls threw open the door and started to march over to where Markus was sitting.

"Crap! Uh, uh..."

He glanced about. There wasn't much time, and the van ride hadn't left Markus in a particularly clearheaded state. A dozen ridiculous ideas floated through his brain. He could bonk the lady on the head and be gone by the time she woke up, but assaulting the elderly wasn't high on his list of valid solutions. He could throw a tarp over Blodgette and pretend she was a piece of machinery, but that would require things like getting Blodgette to understand she needed to stand still, keeping the old lady from actually looking under the tarp, and *having* a tarp to throw over her.

In the end, he decided to do what had worked for five-year-olds for hundreds of years.

"Run! Hide!" he yelped.

He rushed to Blodgette and tugged her arm, "helping" her to her feet as best he could. She didn't quite understand what was going on, but had a firm enough grip on the concept of abject panic to realize that if Markus was running from something, she should run too.

The pair sprinted into the forest. At least, Markus sprinted. Blodgette's locomotion was better suited to verbs like "thundered" or "chugged." She wasn't built for speed, but once her pudgy legs got her moving she quickly transitioned from "immovable object" to "irresistible force." Trees swayed and trembled as she thumped by. Bushes unfortunate enough to be in her path were utterly flattened.

A small gulley lay ahead, a few dozen steps away. Over the rumble of Blodgette's strides he could just hear the babbling of a small brook. As they crested the hill between them and the brook, Markus slid to a stop and dropped down. Blodgette charged by him, noticed he was missing, then skidded to a stop and plodded back.

"Down! Down!"

The previous lesson still fresh in her mind, Blodgette was happy to oblige. She plopped to a seat again, dislodging one of the smaller branches from a nearby tree. It thunked down beside her.

Markus crawled up the hill and peeked over the side. Blodgette's path of destruction was hard to miss, tracing a line of craterlike footprints and pummeled greenery right to their hiding place.

"Craaaaaap. We may as well have drawn her a map. She's going to find us," he hissed to himself.

The woman rounded the corner and took a step back. She kicked one of the five-gallon jugs, then gave a wary glance at the devastation leading into the woods. She murmured something too quiet to be heard, then looked nervously in their direction before retreating back toward the garage.

"What? Why would she... heh... heh heh..." Markus laughed deliriously. "She thought you were a bear or something. And because she's not a crazy idiot like me or Gale, she actually knows to stay *away* from large, dangerous animals. I guess no amount of planning trumps dumb luck, huh, Blodgette?"

He turned. Now that the impromptu game of Let's Do What Markus Does had concluded, Blodgette's fascination with the nature she'd seen so little of had returned. She had climbed to her feet and waddled over to the brook. A tentative toe in the water convinced her it wasn't something horribly destructive or dangerous, so she waded in and flopped down again, splashing about like a toddler in a kiddie pool.

"Good, good. That's fine. Now, you just stay here. I'll see if I can fetch the bottles and fill them up here."

He stood and took a step. By the time he'd reached the top of the hill, he had a soggy, enthusiastic pizza dragon beside him again.

"... Or we can just wait here until Gale gets back..."

#

In Italy, Dimitrios had his feet up on a table that, unbeknownst to him, cost more than the remaining mortgage on his house. It was the centerpiece of an office that a family of four could comfortably live in, and, aside from serving as a footrest, also held a tray of fruit and cheese.

"You've got some excellent wine, Hearst," he said, sipping at his third glass.

"I'm pleased you approve," Hearst said.

The tycoon sat at a large desk with an excessively modern design. He was working diligently on a thin, silvery laptop and taking an endless series of calls. The phone on the desk rang and he snatched it up.

"Yes… yes. Excellent. Make the information available to Ms. Grumman. Thank you. Yes. Yes, I see the attachment. Good work." He hung up. "Mr. Spiros, I—"

"Dimitrios."

"Dimitrios, I have a team of experts who have assembled a short list of questions regarding the history of our mutual point of interest. I wonder if you would be willing to answer a few more questions. I shall record the answers for analysis."

"You keep the wine flowing and I'll answer anything you want!" he said.

"Yes…" He clicked the record button and took a seat beside Dimitrios. "We shall begin with the most pertinent question, and I urge you to be honest with me in light of the significant sum of money I have already paid you. Do you have any idea where the *Structophis gastrignae* is right now?"

"Haven't a clue," he said, taking another sip.

"And you realize that the conditions of our agreement stipulate that full payment is contingent upon the timely retrieval of the creature?"

"We'll find it. The thing can't have gone far. It's huge. Maybe it just wandered off."

"The lack of significant news or police attention in the area would suggest otherwise. We shall set that point aside for now and focus instead on those things that will help us to identify it."

"That shouldn't be too difficult either. It isn't as if there're pizza dragons roaming the streets to get it confused with."

"Nevertheless, I've found more information is always superior to less. As I understand it, you misplaced the literature associated with the *Structophis gastrignae* at some point, which had the mixed blessing of bringing you to my attention."

"Didn't misplace it. Set it on fire. Big difference. Misplacing something is careless."

"Setting aside the fact that you have misplaced the entire creature, is immolating something somehow *not* careless?"

"Nah. That's just putting it in the wrong place at the wrong time when fire is part of the mix."

"A nuanced distinction. At what point in the creature's development did this occur?"

"It was after it hatched but before it came out of the oven. Probably about four years ago."

Hearst nodded. "And how well versed were you in the care of the creature at that level of development?"

"What's to know? You shovel in chunk charcoal in the morning and sweep it out at night. It's a real pain, mind you. I learned that once Markus lost his nerve."

"Yes, Markus..." Hearst tapped the name into his computer. "Once again, that would be your great nephew?"

"That's him. He's the only other person I trusted to do the shoveling. Loads of people would have been *eager* to steal a great idea like a pizza dragon mascot. You want someone you can trust, keep it in the family."

"A fine policy. As the primary care until the true emergence is entirely limited to cleaning and feeding the incubation oven, is it fair to say Markus was the primary caregiver?"

"Again, until he up and quit. Started going to school for maintenance or something."

Hearst tapped some more. "Veterinary medicine."

"Same thing. That's maintenance for animals."

The mogul leaned aside and tapped his intercom. "Get me an update on Markus Spiros."

"Veterinary medicine..." Dimitrios mused. "Handy, really. Probably should have given him a call when the thing started busting out of the oven. He might have been able to help, and it would have saved me a plane ride. ... Eh, next time. Say... I think I still had him as my emergency contact for this little project. I'll bet *he's* got the dragon."

"Yes, Dimitrios, this was established almost immediately upon your involvement, you'll recall."

The voice of Hearst's secretary interrupted his monologue. "I'm afraid there was still no answer at the home number or the mobile, and the last contact with friends, family, and acquaintances was a series of calls to his aunt and the visit to the bistro. We are attempting to gain access to local law enforcement, but our field team in Colorado is limited."

"Stay on it," Hearst said. "Dimitrios, with his background in veterinary medicine, do you believe Markus would know what treatment was necessary for the *Structophis gastrignae?*"

"Probably. He's a sharp cookie."

"And do you believe he would endeavor to provide it?"

"Sure. He'd do anything for his ol' Great Uncle Dimitrios."

"That the *Structophis gastrignae* hasn't shown up in the news suggests he demonstrates a keener understanding of the legal issues of this matter than you. Fortunate for us in that it retains the possibility of the surreptitious acquisition of the creature, but it does complicate its location."

"Sir," interjected the secretary again, "we have an identification on the female who was seen with Markus Spiros as well as the vehicle used."

"Excellent."

"The woman is a graduate student, Gale Dekker. Former classmate of Markus, currently pursuing a degree in zoology. Focus on exotic megafauna. Her name is on six waiting lists for *Structophis gastrignae* research."

Hearst raised an eyebrow. "Excellent work. That is exceedingly relevant. And the vehicle?"

"It was the catering truck registered to the business. We have distributed a description and the license number to the field team."

"Fine work. Though with a five-hour head start, we may need to cast a very wide net to locate it. I trust you have already placed inquiries into any research and treatment centers with the facilities to care for a *Structophis gastrignae?*"

"Yes, sir. No positive responses, but we are still awaiting answers from three of them."

"Splendid work. Keep me posted." Hearst leaned forward and folded his hands on the desk. "Dimitrios, given your lackadaisical relationship with details and precision, I think it is safe to assume that the years in your care may have left the specimen somewhat the worse for wear. Now that we know it is currently in the possession of not one but two people with at least partial training in animal care, I think we can *also* safely assume they will take actions to correct any health issues that may have resulted from your mishandling. For that reason, knowing the precise nature of your mishandling could be crucial in determining their current location."

"I was doing just fine. The thing was the size of a cow. Bigger, maybe. Hard to tell when it's standing up..."

"We'll start with the oven. Where did you acquire the clay and bricks for the oven, and what size did you build it?"

"Pff. Clay and bricks. We don't do any of that trendy art-house cooking. Good old-fashioned deck ovens. Two of them. About... call it six feet tall. Maybe four feet wide and four feet deep."

"As I understand it, that is not a suitable choice."

"It is when you want it to be a mascot for your not-at-all-brick-oven bistro."

Hearst shut his eyes. The faintest flutter of his nostrils served as the only evidence of his mounting frustration.

"Let us move on, shall we? Post-emergence, it is extremely important to have a source of water to help regulate temperature. Did you have the foresight to have a pool or large tub accessible to the creature?"

"See, now that's the sort of thing that would have been useful to know. That's the sort of stuff I came here looking to find out."

The mogul shut his eyes again and stifled a fresh tremor of irritation. "You *are* aware that the terms of our agreement require you to hand over a healthy and thriving creature, are you not? At this rate it does not sound as though this creature is going to survive long enough for my associate to arrive in the United States to supervise its final acquisition."

"Bah. I'm sure Markus and that girl are doing an excellent job of taking care of our investment..."

***

"Keep pushing!" Gale grunted.

In hindsight, their current predicament was entirely predictable, if perhaps not entirely avoidable. Once Gale returned with a fully fueled van, a few bundles of firewood for Blodgette to snack on, and a bag of hoagies, they had to load up and head out. Blodgette treated the prospect of climbing back into the truck with the same enthusiasm as a dog being loaded into a pet carrier in preparation of a vet visit. Unlike a dog, however, that she outweighed the largest of her caretakers by easily a factor of five meant she was far better equipped to resist.

At the moment she had propped a hand against the two top corners of the van's rear doors, and her legs were hooked over the rear bumper. Gale and Markus each had their shoulders against her chest, pushing and shoving with all their might. They were doing a better job of getting the van rolling than actually getting Blodgette inside.

"It'll be fine, Blodgette. Honest. If you want, I'll drive. *Please want that!*" Markus said.

The dragon's only response was an obstinate chirp every time either of her keepers shoved.

"Okay, okay," Gale said, giving up on the shoving for a moment.

She took a seat on the bumper. Markus sat beside her, and after it became clear they were no longer trying to load her inside, Blodgette settled down beside them. She wrapped her arm around Markus, because heaven forbid he have a few minutes of *not* being constricted by her poorly calibrated affection.

"You know, if you and your uncle had been raising her properly, she'd have a much better understanding of the language and we could probably just talk her into getting inside," Gale said.

"*I'm* not thrilled about getting back inside. I don't think language is the issue here," he said.

"Okay, fine. I'm a bad driver. I'm a city girl. It's mostly busses and cycling for me. But that doesn't help us right now, does it? And we've got to hurry. The sun's getting ready to set, and if you don't like my day driving, you're going to hate my night driving."

"Not to mention it's only a matter of time before the old lady who runs this place comes out to investigate again. Bear or no bear, she's bound to be pretty curious about a delivery truck from half a state away that's rocking back and forth behind her garage."

"What's this about bears?"

"Never mind. What we *need* is some positive reinforcement, right? A treat or something."

"The wood's already in the back. If she was *that* interested in it, she'd have gone for it by now."

"No, no..." He squinted into the distance. "See that orange flower over there?"

He pointed. She adjusted her glasses and followed his gesture. "There're a bunch of flowers over there. Do you mean the *Sphaeralcea coccinea* or the *Ipomopsis aggregata*?"

He stared at her blankly.

"What?" she said. "I took Ornamental Horticulture as an elective. There aren't *that* many orange flowers in the Colorado mountains, so it's pretty easy to differentiate them at this distance thanks to the elongated—"

"*It doesn't matter,*" Markus hissed. "Go get one of them and bring it over here. Blodgette likes flowers."

"She does? That's great!" Gale said, digging for her notebook. "She should start developing interests and potential hoarding behavior soon, and flowers are a strong indicator that she'll start—"

A door in the distance opened. The owner of the garage was heading back out.

"Notes later," Gale said, stowing the pad.

She rushed toward the flowers, and the very moment she tugged them from the ground, Blodgette took a dedicated interest in what she was up to. The dragon heaved herself to her feet, nearly causing the van to wheelie, and took Markus by the hand to plod along toward Gale.

"Excellent. *Excellent.* This is a wonderful sign of proper intellectual development," Gale said, carefully sidestepping the interested creature so that she could climb into the rear of the van.

Blodgette followed her right up to the doorway, then hesitated.

Markus glanced behind them. The woman was in plain sight now. She must have been badly nearsighted, or else she'd have been running and yelling already, but their luck wouldn't hold out much longer.

"Come on!" Markus said, trying to sound more encouraging than panicked. "Let's go look at those flowers. Those are *orange* flowers. You've never smelled an *orange* flower before."

He stepped inside. Blodgette tried to tug him back out.

"Oh? You don't want them?" Gale said, waggling the little bouquet. "Then I guess I'll just keep them for myself…"

She motioned as though she was going to tuck them into her pocket. This was the last straw. Blodgette ducked her head and climbed into the van to grab the flowers. As she sniffed happily at them, Markus reached back and slammed the rear doors.

Blodgette turned to look at them, then quickly whipped her head back around to see Gale slipping through to the driver's seat. The pizza dragon narrowed her eyes and glared at Markus, warbling a chirp of betrayal.

"I'm not any happier than you are, Blodgette, but it's for your own good," he said. "And *mine*, since I can't imagine she wouldn't call the cops on me."

"Okay, I'm going to try to make it before sundown, and that means I'm going to have to pick up the pace, so things might get a little bumpier."

Gale started the engine and set about getting it into gear. Blodgette whimpered. Markus spread his arms in preparation for the comforting embrace the dragon would need.

"Let's do this," he said.

The dragon dropped the flowers and hugged him tightly as Gale peeled off onto the road.

***

"That's right! You get out of here, you hooligans!" called the garage owner as the poorly parked and highly suspicious truck sped off.

She took a look around, muttering to herself all the while.

"Rotten teenagers think they can park their ol' jalopies here, like I won't see 'em. Probably want to drink their beers and smoke their doobies without the police knowing any better, then leave a mess all around for decent, hardworking people to clean up."

Her investigation failed to turn up any offending drug or alcohol paraphernalia. There *was*, however, a mangled yield sign tossed into the brush beside the garage.

"Vandals. I suppose *these* hooligans were fine with just tearing up my nice, neat soil with their party vans and wrecking city property or... *well*... what have we here?"

She crouched down and looked over one of Blodgette's footprints. "Looks kind of small to be a bear... but deep. Whatever it was, it must have been a *heavy* one. Ignorant kids don't even know how close they came to being some big critter's *lunch*. Good riddance, that would have been." She turned back and headed for her office again. "But I can't be doing business with a big ol' critter traipsing about. Better go see what's what so's I can let the animal-control folks know what they're dealing with."

She made her way back to the office and unlocked the door to a dusty back room. Inside sat what was perhaps the *last* VHS tape–based security system in operation. She twisted some knobs and flipped through some different camera views. Wavy, low-resolution footage rolled backward as she nudged switches and turned dials. Eventually she found the best view of where Markus, Blodgette, and Gale had been engaging in their comedy of errors.

The distance, angle, and antiquated technology combined to produce what could charitably be called a "bigfoot-sighting-quality" view of their shenanigans. It wasn't good enough to identify any of the players involved. Mostly it was barely enough to make it clear that one of them was extremely large and extremely not-human.

"What in the world...?" she murmured, squinting at the screen.

She rolled back and forth, eventually watching them lumber out of view. The van jerked and rocked for a while, then finally sped off with no sign of the animal afterward.

The elderly woman pulled out a much-abused yellow pages and flipped through, then punched in the number she found.

"Yeah... Animal control? You might want to send some boys down this way. At first I thought I had a bear problem, but... I don't know. Looks like somebody was stealing a..." She rewound the video. "Heck, it *could* be a bear. Lord knows what *else* might stand on two legs like that. ... Well heck, I don't know. Maybe it's an illegal circus. They must have them. They got an illegal everything else, why not a circus? ... Just send down some boys. You can see for yourself. But *something* fishy is going on, that's for certain."

***

Forty-three minutes later, Gale turned onto the gravel road that, if the navigation app could be believed, would bring them to the quarry-turned-camp-turned-nature reserve. She leaned down to get a better view of the gorgeous vista. Both of its past lives had combined to give it a truly unique aesthetic. Ahead of them, a huge, almost white pit with unnaturally steep sides leading down to a glassy lake marked where the excavators had taken their share of the mountain. Peppered here and there like garnish were elements of the summer camp that it had become, mostly in the form of decorations that were tap-dancing on either side of the ethnic-sensitivity line. Like so many other camps, they'd gone with a Native American theme. Totem poles and other attempts at authentic decoration ranged from merely inaccurate to stunningly stereotypical with brief flashes into a vague racial faux pas or two.

"We're here. You used to spend your summers here?" Gale said.

"For a while."

"Lucky... I can only imagine the sort of wildlife you had access to."

"That was the good part. The bad part was being the kid who was actually *interested* during the nature hikes."

"Oh... yeah... The whole *nerd stigma*. If only those lunkheads who picked on the geeks knew we'd be running things when we grew up."

The road took a turn, and a small guard booth came into view. It was staffed by a thickly built young man with a vacant expression and a handheld game system. When he saw the van, he straightened up and clicked it shut. He didn't seem overly pleased to suddenly have a job to do.

"Speaking of lunkheads... try to keep Blodgette quiet. There's a guard."

"Great..." Markus said.

She slid a flimsy curtain aside to hide the view of the inside of the van and rolled down the window as she pulled up to the steel gate blocking the path.

"Can I help you?" the guard said, his tone restructuring the flavorless recitation into something more akin to *Make it quick.*

"Hi there. I'm a student from down south," she said, digging out her school ID. "Zoology. Got a big research project to do, and this little refuge seems like the perfect place to get it done."

He looked over the ID, then handed it back and reached into the booth to pull out a clipboard with a sparse printout attached. "I don't have anything on the reservation list about a research trip."

"Last minute change of plans. Originally I was going to do a study on the local reindeer ranches, but something *much* better came along."

He glanced at the side of the truck, then back at her. "And it involved a beat-up delivery truck?"

"What, this? … Cheap rental. The guy who runs the place went on a trip. Let me borrow it."

She smiled hopefully and was met with little more than an irritated glare and a heavy silence. The silence was eventually broken by a chirp from Blodgette, followed by the *thwomp* of her denting out the rear door, hoping they were done traveling.

He glanced to the source of the sound, then back at Gale. The smile had turned brittle, and was framed by an anxious expression, but she held it rigidly in place as though no one smiling could possibly be up to no good.

"Let me tell you something," the guard said. "The United States Fish and Wildlife Service pays me barely more than minimum wage to make sure that this little patch of land stays pure."

"It was a quarry and a summer camp. It is the opposite of pure," Gale said.

"*They pay me barely more than minimum wage* to make sure it stays pure," he repeated. "So I could just turn you right around. And I should. Or I could have you open up those doors there so I can make sure you don't have anything that might threaten the environment that they pay me barely more than minimum wage to protect. And maybe I will. Unless something comes along to convince me to skip doing the stuff that they pay me barely more than minimum wage to do."

By the second instance of his not-so-subtle prompting, she was already digging in her pocket for her wallet. She pulled out two twenties and dropped them out the window.

"Oops," she said.

He shook his head. "See, it's littering like that that they pay me to watch out for. Now I'm going to *look the other way* to clean up our pure wilderness. Don't you do anything dishonest while I'm doing it."

The guard reached inside the shack and buzzed the gate open, then leaned down to collect the bribe.

"Well, that went better than expected," she said. "Though this little mission is starting to get expensive. The faster I figure out how to legitimize all of this and get a grant to pay for it, the better."

She rumbled along the increasingly decrepit road toward the lake. It was enormous and, like most man-made things, composed of the sort of straight lines nature tended to forgo. The body of water was perfectly rectangular. Only one corner of it was visible from the road. The rest disappeared behind a thick stand of evergreens. In the distance, more than a half mile away and barely visible, some shadowy cabins, the core of the summer camp, could be seen.

Before long, the road became too rough for even Gale's poor driving instincts. She stopped, threw on the parking brake, and popped the doors open.

"Here we are, everyone."

Blodgette practically catapulted herself from the back of the van, hauling Markus along with her like a rag doll. What at first seemed like a desperate bid for freedom soon revealed itself to be a rabid enthusiasm for the shimmering body of water ahead.

"No, no. No, no, no, no, Blodgette—I don't want to go swimming, don't!"

SPLASH!

Gale smiled and crossed her arms, watching as Blodgette rolled to her back and drifted along in the frigid water, Markus gasping from the cold and sputtering beside her. She grabbed her camera and snapped a few pictures while there was still light enough to do so.

Markus climbed up on top of Blodgette like a raft and shook the water out of his hair. "Well... *somebody's* happy to be here," he said.

Blodgette trilled happily and dunked her head back to gulp up some water and release a steamy sigh of contentment.

"Now *that's* what a happy, healthy *Structophis gastrignae* looks like." Gale rubbed her hands together. "Now let the *real* research begin."

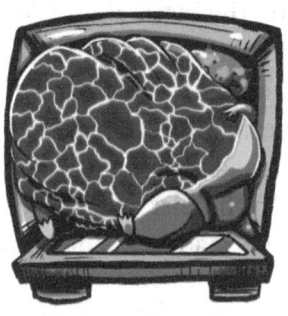

Chapter 6

Pizza dragons, a bit like hermit crabs, instinctively use their surroundings to craft a protective covering. In the case of pizza dragons, it is a much more permanent choice, swiftly becoming a physical part of the beast. Though it changed from beast to beast, most of the creatures crafted something of a mask out of their former home. With so much of communication coming from facial expressions, one would have imagined this would make the emotional state of such a creature more difficult to read. For Blodgette, at least, nothing could be further from the truth. Ever since she'd arrived at the quarry lake, her body language had been screaming relief, excitement, and contentment.

A nice long swim in the lake had cooled her off, and now as the air was dipping down to a genuine chill, she was tottering around the shore of the lake investigating anything and everything. Gale followed along, the light from her phone supplementing the fading evening glow as she recorded video and narrated.

"As you can see, the specimen is heeding her instincts. We are at an old quarry, right at the edge of the pit. The stones here are mineral rich, and the *Structophis gastrignae* is now searching for the essential nutrients that will help her grow, maintain her armor, and otherwise progress to adulthood."

"I feel as if I'm in a nature documentary," Markus said, pacing along beside Blodgette.

"Shh! I'm narrating," Gale said. "The mechanism by which the *Structophis gastrignae* identifies the composition of the mineral deposits surrounding it is still only weakly understood. It is believed that sophisticated chemical receptors—like a more complex version of taste buds—can be found in both the mouth and inside the 'crop' of the creature. But thus far the specimen has discarded many stones without even tasting them, so there must be a visual, scent-based, or even tactile identification method. Perhaps all three."

"I think she's just looking for shiny ones."

"She's not just looking for shiny ones," Gale hissed. "Our current facility isn't *quite* set up yet. We are missing some key bits of research equipment that I hope to have shortly, but observed behavior has already been extremely educational. As indicated in my written notes, this specimen was raised in near isolation, my research assistant—"

"Is that my official title?" Markus asked. "And here I was thinking you were my accomplice."

"*My research assistant,*" she repeated, raising her voice angrily, "is one of only two individuals who were present during the early life stages, and despite being separated for more than five years, both trust and recognition were nearly immediate. He has been the primary avenue for social and intellectual study. We have so far demonstrated the well-documented capacity for rapid learning, as imitation and simple affection-based rewards asserted themselves organically through normal interaction."

She leaned out from behind the phone. "Do the thing," she whispered insistently. "Like we talked about."

"What? Oh, right." Markus paced out in front of Blodgette. "Blodgette, go like this."

He balanced on one leg, arms held out to either side for stability. Blodgette warbled happily and did the same. She wasn't the most graceful creature, so it took a bit of teetering and a few swishes of her long, chubby tail to get the balance right.

"Good job! High-five!" he said.

She released a scaled-up version of an adorable little peep of excitement and nearly fell over in her eagerness to receive the precious hand slap.

"Remarkable, isn't it?" Gale said. "We are barely twenty-four hours post-emergence. As I've said, Markus is the trusted individual, but in the day we've spent together I believe I have earned a degree of the same trust."

Gale stepped in front of Blodgette, holding out her hand in front of the camera. She cleared her throat.

"High-five, Blodgette."

The dragon looked at her flatly, then plodded in a wide path around her to avoid having to deal with her before continuing her investigation of the surrounding stones.

Markus snickered. "Blodgette, you shouldn't leave Gale hanging."

"Clearly I have more work to do to earn the proper level of trust," Gale muttered.

Blodgette chirped and thudded over to the edge of the water. She scooped up a fist-size stone and brought it over to the light, and thus to the camera. It was gleaming and smooth, with little sparkling flecks throughout. She peeped again, then stuffed it into her mouth to gnaw on.

"She *was* looking for a shiny one," Gale said, more excited than disappointed that she had been wrong. "Well done, Markus."

"Just being the best research assistant I can be."

"I'll have to take samples of rocks like that and figure out how to analyze them. As you can see, rather than the typical ceramic or masonry, this dragon was raised in a steel oven. It is my theory that her tastes will mirror the general chemical makeup of this covering in order to help her organically augment and repair it over time. And on the subject of theories..." She pulled the temp-gun out of her pocket and pointed it at Blodgette. "The specimen is freshly out of a full-body immersion to get her temperature down, but she's still running a bit cooler than one would expect. It could just be the night air and the lower water temperature, but evidence is mounting that the specimen, perhaps as a result of her unique physiology or perhaps simply because of a quirk in her genetics, is able to slightly regulate her temperature even at this young age, and is able to comfortably endure high-er-than-average temperatures at steady state with no signs of discomfort. I hope to determine how precisely this is achieved before the development of her natural heat vents makes that more difficult.

"My battery is getting low, so I'm going to have to end this here, but expect more video logs as we learn more about this astonishing creature." She tapped off the video and pocketed the phone.

"All done with the Animal Planet routine?" Markus asked.

"Don't talk to me about Animal Planet," Gale said. "Ever since they put on that show about tree houses, Animal Planet has been dead to me. But yeah, I'm done with the narration."

"Good, because there's some stuff that needs to be addressed."

"Is there? Blodgette seems to be doing okay. We're far enough off the beaten path that no one's going to spot us without coming all the way into the nature reserve or flying over in a heli-copter. She's got plenty of firewood, and it looks as if she's found some rocks she likes. Oh, but you're right. We should stock up on fixings. Herbs, spices, flour…"

"Yes, we should do that," Markus said, running his fingers through his hair, which was still damp from his impromptu dip. "But there's also us to think about. Or more specifically, me, since I'm the one who isn't going to be able to leave. We left in a hurry. I don't have food, water, toilet paper… I've had to use the bath-room for about nine hours, and the logistics of doing that while being joined at the hip to a pizza dragon have been enough to convince me to hold it, but we're approaching a crisis situation."

Gale blinked. "Okay. A little too much information, but point taken. Let's start making plans for the long haul. We should try to get over to the site of the old camp. See if you can get Blodgette to hop back in the van and we'll—"

Blodgette burbled urgently and flopped down to the ground, digging her pudgy fingers into it like a toddler holding on to a bedspread to keep from being picked up.

"You said the V-word," Markus said.

"Okay, fine. You two start heading over on foot. I'll take the... vehicle out to pick up some supplies. We need food, pizza fixings, clothes for you. Clothes for me too, since I'm not going to have time for a trip home anytime soon... bedding... This is going to be a pretty big bill."

"Once again, I'm going to have to figure out how to heed the call of nature while a metric ton of clingy dragon hovers nearby, so no one's getting off easy."

"Noted. We'll settle up later. Here's my messenger bag. There're some of the textbooks and some granola bars in there. Good luck with your little challenge. Stay away from any three-leafed vines for... you know."

"Uh-huh. Just hurry back."

Gale jogged back to the van and hopped in. She spun the tires a bit before the van lurched forward and skidded to a stop again.

"Seriously, Gale. How did you not get pulled over during the whole trip?"

"Fortune favors the bold."

"Maybe fortune does, but the highway patrol doesn't."

"Then I guess I just got lucky." She spun the tires again for a moment, then eased forward with a bit more control. "There we go. See you in a bit."

She finally got the vehicle moving on the less-than-optimal road surface and was on her way. The much-abused van rattled along toward the gate, leaving Markus and Blodgette alone with only the moon for light.

The dragon watched the hated vehicle retreat into the distance, then looked about with steadily increasing confusion and concern. She chirped and trilled inquisitively. Markus gave her a quizzical look.

"Oh, I see. You don't trust her enough to return the high five, but you don't want to see her go. You're going to have to make up your mind about her, because in the *best* case she's going to be around for a while. In the worst case, I'm going to get locked up and you're going to end up with whoever ends up caring for dragons who have been taken into federal custody."

A stiff wind rushed across the quarry. When it hit Markus's damp skin, it felt as though it blew right through him. He was a lifelong Colorado native, and the thin air of the mountains was a whole different type of cold than the sort of thing people at the coasts had to deal with. For the most part he was used to it, but wet clothes on a cool night still made his teeth chatter.

Blodgette was still staring at him expectantly, as though he could make Gale magically appear without the evil van. When she saw the way he shook when the wind blew, she placed a hand on his shoulder, then quickly pulled it away. A bit of looking back and forth between her hand and his shoulder, followed by a few experimental pokes and prods, established that yes, Markus really was that cold.

She decided that simply would not do and pulled him close to her. The toasty warm skin and armor felt... frankly, wonderful. It took the chill of the air away instantly.

"Much obliged, Blodgette. But we're going to need a better solution. If you're willing to spare some of your snack stash of firewood, I think we should try for a campfire." He fidgeted a bit. "But first... I've got something to take care of."

***

Dimitrios paced back and forth, admiring the decor. His business had technically concluded with Hearst earlier that evening. Far from the sort who would let a good thing go without a fight, after learning that Hearst had brought an associate along with him to send to the United States to oversee operations there, he'd gently suggested perhaps he could hitch a ride back as well. And since he wouldn't have anywhere to be in the hours prior to the departure of the private jet, why not remain with Hearst and continue to exploit his hospitality? Hearst had relented in much the same way one might give up on trying to take something away from a screaming toddler.

Now they were each in the "entertaining room" of his Italian estate, or at least one of them. The longer Dimitrios spoke to this man the more impressed he became with the utter extravagance of his lifestyle.

"So, you spend much time in Italy, Donny?" he asked, leaning in to investigate a piece of wooden artwork hanging on the wall.

"Not typically for more than a few hours, I am sorry to say," Hearst said, thumbing through a stack of reports.

As he finished them, he fed them into a shredder he'd had placed beside him.

"But you've got a house here?"

"Hearst Limited maintains guest residences in most urban centers. We are a multinational organization after all. My primary residence is in Berlin, but I cannot remember the last time I spent more than a week there. Such are the challenges of my chosen management philosophy. I endeavor to stay personally abreast of all crucial matters."

"Oh, sure. You've got to keep an eye on the employees. Wouldn't want them raiding the till."

"It isn't quite so simple as that, but the sentiment is broadly similar."

"So what do you call this thing?" Dimitrios asked, scraping at the framed wooden piece with his fingernail.

Hearst looked up. "That is a piece of intarsia made from Enlightenment-era church pews."

"Intarsia. Sounds contagious," he said, wiping his hand on his shirt.

He continued to pace, eventually coming to a darkened doorway. When he stepped through, the lights automatically clicked on to reveal what looked like something from a natural history museum exhibit. At least seventy different animals stood in breathtakingly natural positions, most prepared with a level of taxidermic skill that made one nervous they might move at any minute.

"Whoa..." Dimitrios said. "You've got a thing for dead animals, don't you?"

"I find the myriad forms nature has attained to be truly worthy of our admiration. They serve as inspiration. Seldom can science expect to do any better than replicate what nature has achieved on its own."

Dimitrios scratched his head and walked past a carefully arranged diorama of bears and elk.

"And you need them to be stuffed and standing in your den to do that?"

"One never knows when inspiration may strike. It is best to perpetually surround oneself with things to nurture the mind at all times."

He stopped in front of what might have been a chicken with a pituitary disorder and the wrong sort of head.

"I've seen this one before. What do you call it?"

Hearst wearily turned. "Ah, so *this* is where it is kept. That, Dimitrios, is the only known complete stuffed dodo. The last of them was thought to have been destroyed some years ago, and museums have been making do with specimens assembled from several different animals. I was able to locate a collector who had a previously unknown one and convince him to part with it. I'd forgotten which of our properties housed it."

"Sounds like the sort of thing you should really donate to a museum then, if they don't have one. Let all the kiddies see it. You could probably make some money on attendance fees, or at least get a fat write-off. Plus the little bronze plaque with your name on it."

"Though I value the work museums do, I personally feel that the great minds of the world can do more good when properly immersed in their chosen inspirations than the general public will if given the chance to blindly wander by the wonders of nature. The mere *chance* that having a dodo in my home might spark a notion that, in five years, could produce a revolutionary new jet engine to speed travel and decrease fuel consumption is reason enough to keep it to myself, wouldn't you say?"

Dimitrios shrugged. "You're the guy with the money. If you're willing to pay, no reason you shouldn't get whatever you want."

"Precisely my sentiment."

He continued looking over the room. As larger and more exotic creatures in the skillful poses that made them look so vibrant and alive filled his view, a thought fluttered up to the top of his mind.

"Say... What exactly are you planning to do with the pizza dragon once you get it?"

"That is none of your concern, Dimitrios."

"I'd still like to know. It's technically my property still."

"No, Dimitrios, it is not. Legally it was never your property, and the contract that it now seems you did not devote the proper amount of diligence to explicitly relinquished any custody rights to my organization. Again, your lack of attention to detail, even when dealing with binding documents, may offer some explanation for your limited success in the business world."

"I've done very well for myself. I'd still like to know. You can't simply leave me out of that particular decision."

"I invoke Article Seven, Paragraph Three of the agreement. If I paraphrase slightly, 'I am the guy with the money, I can do whatever I want.' As you have observed, this is broadly true in life, and specifically true in this exchange."

"But we're partners!"

"I would not characterize our association as a partnership."

"You just paid me fifteen million dollars. That makes us partners."

"No, Dimitrios, that makes you an exceptionally overpaid employee."

Dimitrios felt a spark of irritation at the tone of the statement. Alas, his mind had but a single track, and he held to his bitter feelings only as long as the next interesting event, which followed barely a minute later. In this case it was the familiar voice of Hearst's secretary.

"Mr. Hearst, Ms. Grumman is approaching your door."

The voice came from his phone on the end table beside him, issuing forth despite the lack of any ring or other notification. He tapped the screen. "Yes... yes, of course, send her in," Hearst said.

"Right away, sir."

He tapped the screen to end the "call." Dimitrios checked his watch.

"Doesn't that girl ever get to the end of her shift?" he asked.

"I employ a pair of twins, headquartered in Auckland, New Zealand, and Seville, Spain. They operate on opposing twelve-hour shifts. I find the consistency of communication helps streamline my thought processes."

"... That's rich-man thinking right there. You're a real visionary."

"I like to think so. In a moment you will be meeting an associate of mine. Her name is Ruth Grumman and she is one of my more... *motivated* employees. I allow her to operate with a fair amount of autonomy, as she is often tasked with performing certain necessary evils that might prove difficult for our public relations department to smooth out should they be linked to me directly."

"So she does the dirty work, huh? Strike busting? Rough negotiations? Hostile takeovers?"

"Something like that. From this point forward you will be working directly with her. I have placed her in charge of the acquisition of the *Structophis gastrignae*—"

"Gesundheit."

"—and she may have some additional questions for you. I would appreciate it if you were forthcoming. That will help things go smoothly."

"Fine, fine. My life is an open book."

"Splendid."

The door to the den clicked open and a woman stepped inside. She certainly made a formidable first impression. Her jawline was sharp and strong, her hair a ruthlessly precise crew cut. Similar precision had been applied to the cut of her business suit, the lines of her makeup, and the rigidness of her posture. Overall she gave the impression of someone for whom calipers were a part of her morning grooming.

"Herr Hearst," she said, clicking her heels together in a decidedly military way at the salutation.

"Ms. Grumman. This is Mr. Spiros."

"Dimitrios, please! Why all the formality?" Dimitrios said, jumping to his feet and offering a hand.

"We are German," she said, her accent so crisp it may as well have had corners. "Formality is a matter of personal pride."

"Well, I don't have any of that."

She looked him up and down; her expression made it clear to all but him that he'd been judged and found wanting.

"Don't have any what, Herr Spiros? Formality, or personal pride?"

"Hah! She's a pip, this one!" he said, slapping her on the back.

Somehow, without any discernible change, her expression shifted from disdain to outright murderous rage.

"Yes. A pip." It was less a comment as a hiss of venting steam.

"Ms. Grumman, have you been through the briefing materials?"

"I have, Herr Hearst, and I have already been in contact with the team in Colorado." She glanced to Dimitrios, then back to Hearst. "I do not feel comfortable discussing the further details of my preparations in front of Herr Spiros."

"We're all friends here, right?" Dimitrios said.

"There is nothing about that statement that approaches accuracy, Herr Spiros," Grumman said.

"What have you done regarding a holding facility for the specimen?" Hearst asked.

"We have temporarily acquired a hangar at Denver International Airport and secured it with adequate containment and maintenance facilities. We have also acquired a large, secure cargo van and outfitted it with restraints, a coolant system, and storage for support and monitoring equipment. It is en route to the last known location of the specimen where it will meet with the local team. The private jet currently being fueled for my departure has adequate cargo capacity for the estimated size of the creature."

"Excellent. Have you got any questions for Mr. Spiros?"

She looked to Dimitrios. "I have very little confidence that Herr Spiros will be able to provide any valuable insight."

"We'll have plenty of time for it on the plane anyway," Dimitrios said.

Ms. Grumman shuddered. "Yes… Lamentably so…"

***

Markus and Blodgette paced along around the edge of the quarry lake. He'd just completed what he hoped would stand for a long time as the most surreal and embarrassing moment of his life. Not to put too fine a point on it, it had involved several broad leaves and the constant, vigorous instruction for Blodgette not to turn around. The endeavor had taken them deeper into the night, and had also required that he make his way at least far enough into the forest to convince him there weren't any unknown observers with binoculars peeping on him while he took care of business. It wasn't a rational fear, but reason and logic had been failing him of late.

While he was now greatly relieved, he'd also spent enough time to allow the night to harden and darken further. Even the moon had adopted the nasty habit of passing behind clouds now and again. At those times, the only hint of light came from its veiled glow and the luminescent embers of Blodgette's eyes.

The pair thumped and crunched through the brush. Blodgette held his hand and allowed herself to be led, but the tightness of the grip and the odd peep and trill of concern revealed that some combination of the darkness and the wilderness had put her on edge. She carried the bulk of their equipment, which was just as well, because their "equipment" was mostly bundles of firewood for her to snack on. Three of the bundles were curled in her tail. The last was under her arm. It would seem she was a nervous eater, because every few minutes she would duck her head down and chomp on to the end of a piece of wood, sliding it free from the bundle to gnaw on like an oversize cigar until it had sparked and flared its way down her infernal gullet.

She'd just finished her sixth chunk of wood when the rattle of a branch caused her to abandon the handgrip for a one-armed hug that brought them to a halt.

"It's okay, Blodgette. It's okay," Markus said, gently pushing her away—which is to say, heaving as hard as he could and barely budging her. "We'll be to the camp complex soon. I think. Frankly, hiking was a lot easier when there were paths. And flashlights. And camp counselors. Right about now I'm wishing I'd had the foresight to get my phone back from Gale so I could use the light on it. Anyway, we should be leaving the forest any minute, and then it'll be a straight shot to the buildings."

Blodgette reluctantly downgraded the hug to a handhold again and they continued. They crunched through a few more paces of underbrush before another distant crackle of branches brought them to a halt again. This time Markus heard it too. He held still and scanned the surrounding forest. He couldn't see anything worrisome, though in this darkness an elephant could have been standing a stone's throw away and he wouldn't have noticed it.

"Let's, uh… let's walk a little faster, okay?" Markus said.

The dragon wasn't as obliging as he would have hoped. Her eyes were wide, throat fluttering in a constant low warble of concern. After they'd gone a dozen more paces, the trees thinned a bit and they stepped out into what he'd hoped was the clearing around the lake. Instead it was an unexplained strip that was free of trees. It wasn't until the moon slid out from behind the clouds again that he realized what it was.

"That's a telephone pole. And that's another one. This is great! This'll lead us right to the camp. I forgot this was here!" He took a step but found Blodgette wouldn't budge again. "Come on, Blodgette, we're almost... oh..."

This time, the dragon had good reason to be frightened. Behind them, barely visible at the edge of the trees on either side, were three sets of greenish-orange eyeshine. One set moved closer. A wolf stepped out into the light of the moon.

Markus hadn't spent much time imagining what wild wolves might look like, but if you'd asked him, he would have envisioned a dog. Now that he was staring one down, it was clear that a dog was a dog and a wolf was a wolf. It was not just a matter of scale, although the beast eyeing him up was larger than any house pet *he* had ever seen. It was a matter of, for lack of a better word, intensity. When a dog looks at you and thinks, *Oh boy! Dinnertime!*, it means something entirely different than when a wolf looks at you with the same thought.

"Oh... right... A nature reserve is going to have nature in it..." Markus muttered. "Blodgette, we're just going to hurry up along this clearing here. Maybe swing that tail of yours a lot to keep them at bay. Understand?"

In response, Blodgette released his hand, and a quiet rattling sound rang out beside him. He turned to find that she'd gone "full turtle" again, ducking as best she could into the approximate shape of the former pizza oven and stuffing as much of her doughy flesh behind its ragged steel plates as she could.

"Blodgette? Now's not the time to hide."

The other two wolves slid from the shadows. They were smaller than the first, which mostly meant they were merely frightening and not nightmarish, but that hardly improved the situation at all.

"Okay, Markus. You've been to veterinary school. You've had zoology classes. What do we know? Wolves... uh... pack hunters. They hunt in stages. Locating prey, done. The encounter. In progress..."

The wolves stalked closer.

"Time's running out, Markus. What happens during the encounter? Crap, this was during Professor Medford's class, wasn't it? That guy was *terrible*. Okay, okay... uh... oh, prey response! There's stand ground, attack, or flee. Wolves shouldn't attack unless we flee. You're physically imposing enough to keep them at bay. All we have to do is make sure we don't run."

Blodgette's head perked up. Now *that* was a word she knew. She'd just learned it at the rest stop earlier that day. Run. She could do that.

She unfurled herself and took off at a sprint, lumbering up to top speed in a few strides. Markus realized what she was doing a split second before the wolves did. He took off after her and closed the gap quickly. The wolves dashed after them, spreading into a coordinated attack formation like some sort of woodland fighter pilots.

Now that his flawless plan of "don't do anything and hope for the best" was dashed to pieces, Markus was left in a tug-of-war between the fight and flight flavors of his instincts. Blodgette was lodged firmly in "flight," and momentum trumped tactics, so flight it would be. But as Markus scrambled up onto the base of her tail and climbed up to ride her piggyback, his mind was awash with every nature documentary he'd ever seen, which inevitably included footage of a pack of wolves taking down something many times their size. He wasn't sure they'd be able to cope with the sizzling heat or steel armor Blodgette was sporting, but they would sure as heck be able to pluck off the juicy little pile of meat clinging to her back.

It was too late to stop and face them down. The first steps of their retreat had rung the dinner bell. Maybe if Blodgette had the courage or knowledge to actually fight them, they'd have a chance. But if Blodgette was spooked by a grad student with a camera, she wasn't likely to go mama bear on a pack of wolves anytime soon. As she thundered through the forest with her armor jingling and big hunks of wood slipping from her tightly clenched tail, she was still a good deal more frightening than anything the wolves were likely to have encountered thus far. That might be enough to keep them safe until they reached shelter.

With her almost precognitive ability to do the opposite of what Markus was hoping for, Blodgette turned toward the trees rather than following the cleared stretch of forest toward the campground. Pine boughs whipped past, slapping Markus in the face as he tried to hold tight. The wolves were getting closer now. Any one of them could easily leap up and try to pull Markus down. He scrambled higher on her back, climbing to her shoulders and leaning down across her long, crooked neck. Maybe if he could steer her, turn her head like a horse, he could get her on the right path. The most obvious place to wrangle her was via the shiny, antler-like steel horns that sprouted from her head. He grabbed hold of one and immediately regretted it. The metal was blazing hot, sizzling his hand as he touched it.

"Ow!" he yelped, almost losing his grip as the pain shot through him.

His cry of pain drew Blodgette's attention. She twisted her head to chirp anxiously at Markus but didn't stop running.

"Blodgette! No, no! Just watch where you're going!" he called.

She turned back to the forest ahead in time to see a stout tree was directly in her path. She tried to stop, but several hundred pounds of panicked dragon is a force in motion that particularly likes to stay in motion. She dug two deep furrows in the forest floor trying to stop, then finally struck the tree at a barely reduced speed. Bark splintered, metal screeched, branches broke, and Markus ejected from her back, tumbling to the ground a short distance away. Adrenaline had him springing to his feet almost before he'd finished rolling.

The wolves slowed and stalked in a circle, keeping their distance as loose branches and crackling frost continued to rain down. Blodgette was dazed from the impact but didn't seem to be hurt.

Markus scrambled up to her and stood between the wolves and the dragon. Bits of his brain reminded him Blodgette had a much better chance of survival against these creatures than he did. It would be *smart* to continue running, to leave the wolves to menace the "injured" prey and potentially ignore him long enough for him to reach the campground. Those pragmatic tactics were utterly drowned out by the much louder demand of his heart and conscience: keep Blodgette safe.

He looked around, trying to search his surroundings for weapons while simultaneously keeping his eye on all three predators as they circled. The tree they'd struck had seen better days even before its collision with the organic freight train that now sat dizzily beneath it. Most of the needles were brown, and the bark flaked easily away. It was standing deadwood, dry as a bone. An idea flickered to mind.

Markus grabbed one of the dislodged boughs covered with dead needles and turned to Blodgette.

"Blodgette, look at me," he said, snapping his fingers. "Remember 'aaahh'? Taking your temperature? Open up and say ahh!"

The dragon was still shaking the cobwebs out, but she mustered a half-hearted "ahh" for Markus. He stuck the dry end of the bough into her mouth. She sputtered and spat, but even the brief exposure to her raging inferno of an internal body temperature was enough to ignite the seasoned wood.

Markus thrust the smoldering, smoking wood at the wolves and they quickly backed away, retreating from the alarming sight and scent.

"Hah! That's right!" Markus said triumphantly. "Fire! Mankind's oldest ally! Tremble before the might of the flame!"

Blodgette blinked and pulled herself to her feet, adding her imposing presence to the intimidation factor of the fire. She glanced back and forth between the fire and the wolves. Again, the surprisingly expressive masked face of the creature began to tell a story. These wolves were scary, but they were scared of *fire*. And fire wasn't scary! If they were afraid of something so simple and so harmless, how scary could they really be?

She scooped up a veritable branch from the ground and nibbled on the end until it sparked to flame, then poked it at the wolves. They scampered backward and watched warily. Blodgette trilled proudly and looked to the wolves again, waggling the branch in their direction.

"Yeah!" Markus said. "That's a high five right there."

He held up his hand and she proudly slapped it, perhaps with a bit more enthusiasm than was called for. After Markus recovered, he squinted into the distance.

"Let's go. It can't be too much farther to get to the campsite. The wolves should back down now, or at least lose interest after a few minutes, but I don't want to press my luck. It'll be tricky enough getting there without burning the forest down."

Blodgette snuck her hand into his and waddled along happily beside him. He winced a bit at her grip. His hand was still a bit tender from touching her antlers.

"We'll have to talk to Gale about that headgear of yours. I think we've figured out what's keeping you cool. I'm sure that'll be good for a whole new *section* of the report she'll be writing."

***

As expected, or at least as hoped for, the wolves decided the armored wielders of fire were more trouble than they were worth with regard to a meal for the evening. Just to be on the safe side, Markus and Blodgette kept their smoky torches until they reached the campground.

"Yeesh, this place has seen better days," he said, stomping out his torch.

Nature was in the process of reclaiming the facility. Most of the smaller cabins—barnlike structures that held the bunks used by overnight campers—were in various states of decay. They'd all been locked with padlocks that were rusting over, and one of them had suffered a roof collapse. The Native American motif with its bright colors had been faded and sun bleached down to something oddly pastel. Signs with instructions and maps were now illegible masses of peeling paint and splintered wood.

"All that's missing is a narration about a masked murderer who went on a rampage twenty years ago, and we'd have a perfect slasher film reboot," Markus said.

There was one building that had seen at least *some* maintenance. That was the main cabin. Three stories high and sturdily built, it looked something like a cross between a log cabin and a public school. They stepped up onto the elevated deck that wrapped around the structure and Markus peered through the windows to the darkened interior. Steel gratings covered them, a semi-recent addition that would make breaking in more of a challenge than he'd hoped.

"I don't see a security system or anything... There shouldn't be an alarm if we manage to get inside," he said. "Back when I was spending my summers here, this was where all the rainy-day activities were. There's a basketball court over there. Sort of a preschool area for the toddlers over there. I think the upper levels had the lodging for the counselors. I was never on the third floor. Probably offices and stuff."

He investigated the door. It had been chained and padlocked as well, but the lock wasn't rusted at all, and there was evidence of a recent repair on the deck nearby. Other places where repair *should* have been done suggested that this place was receiving only the barest of maintenance necessary.

"I guess someone's keeping this place from falling apart. More or less. Probably they use it for administration or something when they need to do... nature reserve stuff." He tugged at the lock. "Give this a good hard yank, would you?"

Blodgette twisted her head, then grabbed the lock and tugged at it.

"Harder. This you can break. And hurry up. I'm not going to assume those wolves are out of our hair for good."

She yanked a few more times, then winced when the chain finally snapped. The lack of a reprimand was met with a sigh of relief, and the pair walked inside. Markus flipped the switch on the wall, but the hallway remained dark.

"That was too much to hope for," he said. "And I'm certainly not going to carry a torch in this place—that's just asking for trouble. Come on. It's been a long time, but I'm pretty sure the supply closet was over this way."

They fumbled their way down a side hallway. Either Markus had misremembered the layout or the place had reorganized in the years since he'd last been there, because as best as he could tell by rummaging around, the closets he found along the way were mostly filled with cardboard boxes packed with executive detritus like clipboards, toner cartridges, and adhesive labels.

"Seems as if this place went white-collar at some point," he mused, checking the latest box in the dim moonlight from the window.

Eventually they found their way to the kitchen, and he checked the cabinets.

"Jackpot. Fully stocked with canned goods." He tested the oven, and while it didn't light, there was the hiss of gas. He quickly shut it off. "Seems as though the propane is stocked up too. Which means there's probably... bingo."

A nearby drawer revealed matches, and another one had candles.

"Let there be light."

He lit a candle for himself and one for Blodgette. Perhaps it was the running or the snacking, but her temperature was running high enough that it got a little soft in her grip, but not unmanageably. Now that he could see, he started looking through the stuff in the cabinets.

"Let's see. Canned white potatoes. Canned beets. Canned corn. Green beans. Oh, hey, tomato puree. Hungry?"

He tossed her the can, and she snapped it up in her mouth like a dog catching a treat. It went over in much the same way, with Blodgette's brief and evident delight followed by an intense interest in having another. Markus obliged, then continued his investigation. Eventually he turned up a logbook in one of the drawers.

"Okay, let's see what we have here." He cleared his throat and began to read. "'Department of Fish and Wildlife, Site 1214 Supply Manifest for Administration Building, May 15.' Seems as though they restocked this place a few months ago. 'Food: 250 cans, nonperishable, including... blah blah blah... 50 hand-crank flashlights with USB chargers.' It'll be handy to find where they're hiding *those*. 'Propane: 850 gallons for heating/cooking. Diesel: 500 gallons for generator.' Cool, if we can find *that*, we'll actually have lights."

As he read off additional potential handy things, like first aid kits, he discovered a section labeled "Service Road Maps."

"What's this now?" he said.

He flipped to the indicated section of the logbook and looked over the simple lines of roads that had apparently been kept up in order to facilitate research and basic maintenance.

"Oh, you've got to be kidding me. If she'd just taken a right instead of a left, there's a service road that goes around the other side of the lake that leads all the way to the parking area right across the courtyard. Too bad I can't call Gale to let her know about that, and our little wolf problem. But... wait a minute... there're *phone* lines. And *someone* is keeping this place stocked with the basic amenities. So in theory..."

He marched to the old-style landline phone on the wall and picked it up.

"Bingo! Dial tone! I can call her! ... Except I don't know her number, it's in my cell phone. Which she has." He slouched. "Stupid technology, robbing me of my memory. Wait, wait... 4-1-1... hah! Thank you Luddites for not trusting the internet!"

Markus navigated his way through a somewhat decrepit automated system until he finally got her number. It turned out to be her *mother's* number, but a little forced polite conversation eventually earned him her current number. He dialed and almost immediately she answered.

"Hello?" she said curiously.

"Gale, it's Markus. I didn't expect you to pick up the phone. Aren't you supposed to be driving?"

"Speakerphone. Where are you calling from?"

"The main building of the camp. It's some sort of an admin building now. Hopefully no one shows up while we're here."

"Well, ideally you'll be there for two years, so that's not too likely, is it?"

"I wouldn't call that ideal, but that's not why I'm calling. It turns out there's a service road around the other side of the lake. Should get the van all the way here."

Blodgette, either irritated that Markus was no longer paying attention to her or perhaps having heard Gale's voice, attempted to shove her head between his face and the receiver and warbled directly into it.

"Is Blodgette behaving herself?" Gale said with a snort.

"Give me a minute, Blodgette," Markus said, pulling the phone aside. "Listen, be careful when you get here. We had a run-in with some wolves."

"Oh, great!"

"... Great?"

"Yeah! I'd heard they were reintroducing the gray wolf to Colorado. It's great to know they're getting a foothold."

"Wasn't *that* great in the moment."

"Well you're fine, right?"

"Fine is a relative term, Gale. 'Had to run from wolves to avoid dying' is the sort of thing that downgrades the average day from 'fine' to 'harrowing.'"

"You shouldn't have run. You should have stood your ground. Wolves are—"

"Easier said than done, Gale!" He shook his head. "Just hurry back, take the road, and watch for wolves!"

"Will do, so long."

"Bye."

He hung up the phone and shook his head again, looking to Blodgette.

"Gotta love her enthusiasm, Blodgette, but I wish she'd shift her focus to be a *little* more practical."

The dragon, having lost interest in the phone, was snooping around the kitchen. Her long neck meant that just a bit of a stretch let her horns brush the low ceiling, giving her a view of the tops of the cabinets and shelves scattered about the room. Something had caught her eye, but her arms were a bit too stubby to reach whatever it was. After some flailing, she gave up and nudged a box down from the shelf with her snout. It spilled, dumping a few dozen hand-crank flashlights across the floor.

Blodgette cringed at the clattering and looked sheepishly to Markus, anticipating a scolding.

"Hey! The flashlights! Good job, Blodgette!"

She hesitantly raised her hand, testing for the obligatory high five of success. He delivered it. She wriggled happily and swiftly knocked down another box.

"No, no, no!" Markus said. "Knocking down boxes is bad in general, but good in this specific case. Come on. Let's find someplace to keep you occupied."

He grabbed a few of the flashlights, cranked two of them up, and replaced their candles with something a little less hazardous. A few twists and turns through the halls, some of which required Blodgette to squeeze through doorways *barely* large enough for her, brought them to what had formerly been the pre-k playroom. It was stacked with boxes, for the most part, but the colorful decorations still hung on the walls, and a large chest of toys sat under the bank of windows facing the road.

"Here we go, Blodgette. Let's see what you make of these."

He started to dump things out onto the floor for her. She immediately worked out that these were for play and plopped down to entertain herself. Before long she'd settled on some oversize wooden alphabet blocks. After she ate two of them before Markus could stop her, he demonstrated stacking them and she latched on to the concept, mounding them into tall towers until they toppled, then clapping her hands and starting again.

Relieved of the burden of keeping her distracted and entertained, Markus sat on the floor and tried to switch his brain off for a moment. When his thoughts instantly turned to the snarl of ill-advised and ultimately doomed decision-making that had brought him here, he decided instead to shift his attention to something that might at least help him deal with the task ahead.

He slipped out one of the books Gale had provided.

"'*The Development and Physiology of* Structophis gastrignae*: A Study.*' Now *that's* a page-turner of a title if ever I heard one." He thumbed through the pages. "Education. *Structophis gastrignae* are imitative learners, and develop habits and skills very quickly. Though their physiology limits their ability to finely manipulate small objects, the presence of opposable thumbs facilitates human-level tool usage. Depending on the level of early development socialization, this tool usage can facilitate communication methods that overcome the lack of vocal range necessary for spoken communication. *Structophis gastrignae* have successfully learned basic sign languages. Many have learned to read, and some have learned to write.'"

Markus watched Blodgette stacking blocks for a while, then stood and rummaged around until he found a picture book.

"Let's just set a baseline, shall we?" He flipped open the book to a large illustration of a cat. "This is a cat. C-A-T. Cat."

He found the proper blocks to spell it out. One by one, he did the same for the other labeled images.

"D-O-G. Dog. B-A-T. Bat. C-O-W. Cow."

Blodgette's face was one of intense contemplation, scrutinizing the images, the words, and the blocks, over and over.

"Okay, now let's try this." He scrambled up the letters, then pointed to the cat, then the blocks. "Spell it."

For a long time she merely stared down at the blocks. Then she took three of them and lined them up.

"No... No, that says 'fub.' We're looking for 'cat.'" He arranged the proper letters. "'Cat.' Now let's try 'dog.'"

Blodgette looked curiously to Markus and moved the letters, one by one, to the dog picture.

"No, that's 'tac.' We're looking for 'dog.' Like this."

He spelled out the word. She looked over the arrangement of blocks again. Suddenly her eyes opened wider, and she almost vibrated with excitement. She tapped the picture of the dog, then the word "dog," then the blocks.

"Yes, those go together," he said, smiling.

She could barely keep her hands steady as she fumbled through the blocks and piled them next to the picture of the bat. It wasn't exactly flawless. The *A* was actually an upside-down *V*, and the *B* was a sideways *M*. But it was far too similar to be a coincidence.

"Good job! Good *job*. That's a double high five!"

A flurry of spelling followed. Some approximations were closer than others, but a bit of searching and a bit of comparison eventually turned up something at least resembling the proper word. Then, just as quickly as the tizzy of learning started, it stopped.

Blodgette's face made her appear to be deep in thought for nearly a minute, her mind churning at something complex. Finally she turned to Markus and chirped. She tapped the word and then the picture of the cat. Then the word and then the picture of the dog. Then, with a metallic clunk, she tapped her own chest.

"What word is for you? Heh. As much as Gale would prefer I tracked down enough letters for *Structophis gastrignae*, let's take the easier choice. D-R-A-G-O-N. Dragon."

She watched the word form, then moved the blocks carefully together and set them aside. Next, she tapped Markus's chest.

"What's the word for me? I'm pretty sure I saw 'boy' and 'man' and a bunch of stuff like that. Tell you what. How about you try to figure it out?"

Getting her to wrap her head around the challenge he was putting forth took a bit more illustration, but before much longer she was leafing through the pages as gently as she could, scrutinizing images and comparing them to Markus.

"You're a quick learner, Blodgette. I can certainly see that. Pretty soon I'll have to watch what I say around you, or you'll start getting the wrong ideas." He flipped through the text looking at images and skimming passages. "Pizza dragons are amazing creatures, that's for sure. I can see why Gale is so head over heels for them. I just don't... I just have to find Dimitrios. This isn't for me. I can't... I've got a life. I was heading in a certain direction, you know? This is more than I bargained for. Already I'm not sure if I'm going to be able to dig myself out of this mess."

Out of the corner of his eye, he could see she had started to select and compare blocks.

"You definitely deserve a shot at a proper life. Frankly, hidden away with me doesn't seem like the one you should be shooting for, and I don't really think it's got a chance to work. But we'll find someone. Someone who knows what he's doing and has all the right training. You're starting to warm up to Gale, right? You don't necessarily need *me*, right?"

Blodgette placed down a third letter and looked expectantly to Markus.

"Let's see what you came up with," he said.

The blocks she'd selected didn't quite spell a word. The last was a sideways *3*. The second wasn't even a letter, it was a circle from the shape blocks. The first was definitely an *M*.

"*M*... That's probably supposed to be an *O*... and a... I guess that's supposed to be..."

He became silent and looked to the page open before Blodgette. It was the page depicting families. On one side was a father with a daughter on his shoulder. On the other was a son holding the hand of his mother. Blodgette tapped the page, then the blocks, then Markus's chest.

"Mom," Markus said, dropping the word like a bomb. "I'm Mom. Wait... wait, wait. Let's give this one a try."

Markus flipped somewhat frantically through the pages until he found an old-fashioned, business-suit-wearing adult labeled "Man." He then quickly assembled the letters on the ground.

"See? Man. See? Right? That's me."

Blodgette critiqued the word and the image, then flipped back to the family page. Again she compared and considered, then plucked the *M* from "man," tossed away the *3*, and replaced it. She then pointed to the page, specifically to the handholding. She then chirped and held his hand.

"... Well... that pretty much settles it. You really know how to play hardball don't you?"

Blodgette raised her hand, ready for a high five. He shook his head.

"No. That one gets a hug."

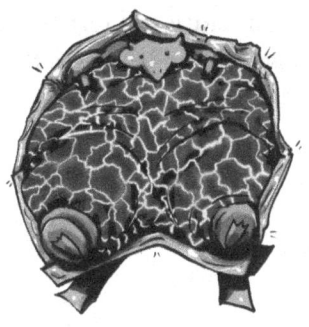

Chapter 7

A private jet cut through the air over the Atlantic. Inside, Dimitrios gazed out the window in the pleasant haze of inebriation that only top-shelf booze can provide. A plane this size would normally have seating for upwards of eighty people, but Hearst Ltd. must have had different requirements for it. The "passenger" section was downright spacious, with seating for four, a full bar, and a small clerical-style desk setup. Ms. Grumman sat at the desk tapping at a keyboard and having angry, pointed conversations with people in at least three different languages.

"Herr Senator, with all due respect, you and I both know that you would not be enjoying your third term if not for the substantial support provided by our mutual acquaintance and his associates. We so seldom ask for you to show your gratitude. It would send a terrible message to deny us so simple a request. ... I appreciate that you do not have any direct authority over the local law enforcement, but a man in your position should be able to exert a certain level of influence over those with the information we require. ... I see. I am sorry to hear that. I shall of course relay this information to my employer. I understand he is presently preparing his annual contribution budget. I do hope this will not influence his future generosity. ... A threat? No, Herr Senator. A threat would be to suggest I might introduce your wife to Ms. Juanita K. Sanchez. I do not believe the two of them have been introduced, despite the many things they have in common. ... I thank you for your consideration, Herr Senator, and our mutual acquaintance does as well." She hung up the phone.

"I've got to say, Ms. Grumman. I'd hate to get on your *bad* side," Dimitrios said, walking unsteadily to the bar to top off his glass.

"If that is so, then you should have been more mindful of your first impression," she said.

"What's that?"

"Nothing, Herr Spiros," she said. "One moment please."

She dialed the phone. "Hello, sheriff's office? Yes, this is Ms. Grumman. I believe you have just received a message from Senator McIntyre's office on my behalf? Good. Very shortly you will be receiving an e-mail from me containing some information I would like you to run through your systems. Please respond promptly with all results you may discover. A telephone number is included in the e-mail. Any calls received from that number should be forwarded to a high-level official, and any time-critical information should be delivered to that phone number as well. Thank you for your compliance."

"This all seems like an awful lot of trouble to go through for an animal. Even a rare one. Are you sure Mr. Hearst would be okay with you leaning on politicians and bossing around the police?"

"Herr Hearst trusts my judgment and has authorized any necessary actions to acquire the creature."

"Anything short of spilling blood, I imagine."

"You imagine incorrectly, Herr Spiros. The usage of force to guarantee success in this or any other endeavor is a lamentable but often unavoidable requirement of the more vigorous negotiation tactics to which I am so often called to attend."

"…But…you won't *hurt* someone over *this*…" Dimitrios said.

"Are you speculating, Herr Spiros, or instructing? Because you are ill-equipped to do either with any level of success."

"I…"

"The question was rhetorical. Now if you will excuse me, I need to report back to Herr Hearst."

She stood without awaiting a reply. A quick code tapped into a door in the rear of the room gave her access to a hallway leading to the back half of the plane.

As the door shut behind her, there were a dozen things that could have been floating through Dimitrios's mind. He could have been having second thoughts about the people he'd chosen to do business with. He could have been wondering just what they had in store for the dragon once they acquired it. He could have begun planning just how he would distance himself from Hearst once the deed was done, or how far he would be willing to help the man before his morals demanded he end their partnership.

What *actually* flitted through his mind, however, was a good deal less complex or impactful. He glanced around to make sure there weren't any video cameras watching him, disregarding the fact that he didn't know what modern surveillance looked like and thus wouldn't be able to spot a security camera even if it was a small black dome mounted in the ceiling two feet from where he was standing. Once convinced he was free to misbehave, he subtly slipped two small bottles of scotch and one bottle of cognac into his jacket.

If he was going to have to endure this rude young woman for an entire plane ride, he was going to make sure it was worth his while.

***

Ms. Grumman stepped into the cargo area of the plane, which occupied its rear third. A large, cruel-looking cage took up a significant portion of the floor, and the walls were covered with various nonlethal equipment. To look at the supplies, one would have thought they were on their way to subdue and capture a dinosaur. She picked up a handset on the wall of the plane and dialed a number.

"Hearst," came the answer.

Grumman replied in German. "All is in readiness, Herr Hearst. I was able to compel the local government officials to give me access to law enforcement systems. I expect to have a definite location of the specimen within the hour."

He answered in German as well. "Excellent. I have had additional briefing on the target. Orders stand as they were: take all necessary actions to acquire it, but the creature is not to be harmed. Achieving this second requirement may prove more difficult than initially thought."

"What is the situation?"

"To the best of our knowledge, no one has ever tranquilized one of these creatures. You've been equipped with the best option our pharmaceutical division could produce, but it is entirely possible that you will have to physically subdue the beast."

"Doing so without injury will indeed be a trying task, sir."

"The experts I have spoken to suggest it may be possible to coax the creature into containment if we can compel an individual who's earned the creature's trust to command or request it to do so."

Her expression hardened. "And I suppose Herr Spiros is the most likely individual currently available to use who might fit that criteria?"

"Indeed. You'll need to keep him with you."

She squeezed the phone tightly enough for its plastic to creak. "How vital is it that the creature be *completely* unharmed..."

"As distasteful as it may be to continue to associate with the boorish Mr. Spiros, the potential earnings of this enterprise justify it. Having the monopoly on discreetly available samples of *Structophis gastrignae* tissue for medical and industrial testing is itself of immeasurable value, but if the creature can be utilized for breeding, we could potentially have an inexhaustible supply of both samples and specimens for usage. Collectors, drug companies, chemical companies, genetics firms. Just imagine the breakthroughs that can be gleaned by a creature able to so efficiently convert fuel into heat. And anyone in the industry who wants to get their hands on it can wait until legislation finally opens the species for study and testing, or they can pay our prices and sign our agreements. Income from the likely patents and discoveries alone are conservatively in the billions. But the creature must be alive and healthy."

"Understood."

"One more thing. It goes without saying that to exploit this creature with any degree of success we will need to prevent the general public and particularly the relevant authorities from learning about it. News has not broken of it yet, so the current keepers may have succeeded in keeping it from public view, but before this operation is through, we shall need to guarantee *their* silence, through contractual or... *other* means."

"Again, Herr Hearst—understood."

"Splendid. Carry on and keep me informed."

***

Nearly an hour of driving in search of a store that was open and could satisfy all their various needs had brought Gale all the way back to the very same rest stop where they'd fueled up on the way to the quarry. The big box store was an all-night affair, and though Gale preferred to help out the mom-and-pop stores, desperate times called for massive multinational conglomerates.

Sure enough, every last item on her list was available for prices that seemed downright unsustainable. Since reception was an iffy thing this far into the mountains, she had taken full advantage of the visit to the nearest vestige of civilization to make some phone calls. Even as she pushed the heavily loaded shopping cart to the rear doors of the van, she had a hands-free headset in place and was wheeling and dealing.

"Hello? Hello, is this Professor Medford? This is Gale Dekker. From class. Yeah, I'm a teacher's assistant in your Wednesday lab. Listen, I was wondering, remember that case in Idaho where the ranch was found to have adopted a pair of endangered caribou, and because the pair had acclimated to their herd, the ranchers were permitted to keep them as long as they had the proper oversight? Yeah. So how does that happen? Is there paperwork, forms you've got to fill out? ... No, I don't. What time *is* it? ... Really?" She checked her watch. "Huh. Time flies. Anyway, so this paperwork... hello?"

She clucked her tongue and tugged the hands-free from her ear.

"Whatever happened to a commitment to excellence, hmm? *This* is why we're having a higher-education crisis right here..."

Gale pulled open the van doors and started to load up the various things she'd purchased, checking them off a mental list.

"Sleeping bags. Toilet paper. Basil. Grated cheese. Whole wheat flour. White flour. Flour for bread makers. Red pepper flake..."

Her brain was, as always, darting in seven directions at once. It juggled the sort of observations she wanted to make sure she was able to make with Blodgette, the various means of legitimizing and extending her research with the beast, working out a better habitat, and dozens of other fleeting notions. Even simple things like the most efficient and secure way to store the groceries so that her unconventional driving style wouldn't threaten them too much. This meant that it wasn't until she was nearly finished loading the groceries—the last of which were an assortment of flowers Blodgette might like—into a carefully secured nest of sleeping bags that she noticed the vehicles across the way.

One was an official van, painted in the bright reflective colors one normally sees on construction vehicles. The words "Animal Control" stretched prominently across the side panel. A pair of vest-wearing animal-control officers stood in the headlights in front of the garage across the street. Two police officers, one a portly woman and the other a gangling man, stood beside a rugged police SUV. The police had their arms crossed and nodded periodically. The rest of the group was engaged in an animated discussion with a very agitated older woman. Gale could only hear snippets of what they were saying, but based upon the hand gestures, the subject of their discussion was very big and lumbering.

Gale felt a flutter of panic in her chest and made ready to slam the van doors. Something caught her eye before she could do so, and a thought came to mind. She shakily snatched a roll of duct tape and threw a few strips over the numbers on the license plate. When the doors were shut and secured, she ran around the front, obscured the front plate, then hopped into the driver's seat.

"It's okay, it's okay. Just play it cool. No one saw you. No one has any reason to suspect you," she muttered to herself.

It was at this point that she heard the first full sentence from the exchange across the street.

"It was a van just like that one!" called the elderly woman.

Gale watched as one of the animal-control officers tried to flag her down.

"Not today, Mr. Authority Figure," she proclaimed, revving up the engine. "Science awaits!"

She slammed on the gas, cringed through a horrible grinding noise, then muscled it into gear and slammed on the gas again. The officer jumped out of the way as she came barreling backward out of the parking lot and squealed out onto the road. Both police hopped into their car. In moments they were on Gale's tail, lights flashing and sirens blaring.

"Oh no you don't. No one gets between Gale Dekker and her thesis!" she cried, riding a wave of adrenaline.

She gripped the steering wheel and made a hard left.

The police had probably had a great deal of training in how to handle a high-speed pursuit. That training certainly had *not* been devised with Gale in mind. For instance, the hard left she took ignored the fact that there was no *road* to the left. She jumped a curb and slung gravel behind her as she crossed an empty lot, heading toward the pine forest in the opposite of an all-terrain vehicle. The police screeched to a halt at the side of the road, then reversed and rumbled after her.

Branches and needles raked across the van as she skidded and slogged through the soft soil between the trees. It was difficult keeping an eye on both where she was going and what the cops were up to, but things became a good deal simpler when a stray branch tore her side-view mirror off and she could devote her full attention to driving. Another driver might have been at her wits' end as the wildly spinning tires failed to provide anything more than a mere suggestion of control and ancient, very solid pine trees rushed by on either side. For Gale, not quite being in control of this lumbering behemoth of a vehicle was par for the course. Without Blodgette and Markus moving around in the back and making their distracting yelps of dismay, it was actually a good deal easier to handle. Thus, while the police gingerly navigated the forest, she blasted through underbrush and drifted down hills until she came to a shallow stretch of the same babbling brook Blodgette had played in earlier.

She splashed through it and made it a few dozen yards up the other side before the muddy ground and threadbare tires proved unable to provide the sort of traction necessary to haul a catering van uphill. No matter. Downhill worked for her. She turned the wheel and splooshed back into the brook, then sped off in the direction of the flow as the police sputtered along on the bank.

"Oh, jeez, I should make sure I'm heading in the right direction," Gale said, her voice not quite achieving the terrified tone her current predicament called for. "As long as I'm in the river, I can probably afford to put one hand on the phone. I just have to steer well enough to keep splashing."

She thumbed her way through menus until she found the history and tapped on the quarry. The screen immediately switched to "Rerouting," so she wedged it into the center console and turned her attention back to the "road." A frightened waterfowl burst from the water just before getting flattened.

"Sorry, duck!" she called, then leaned out the window to watch it take flight. "Wow! A hooded merganser!"

"Pull over! You are in an unsafe area!" bellowed the female officer over the loudspeaker.

"It's not *that* bad. It just a little—*oh my gosh!*"

Ahead, the brook took a sharper turn than the sliding van could follow. Rather than even try, Gale stood on the accelerator, hoping that all of this handy downhill momentum would give her a chance at climbing the slope. It did so and then some, with the van blasting up onto the river-stone bank and then cresting a berm with enough speed to get all four wheels in the air. She knocked some branches off a tree and flattened a sapling, then roared onward through the thickening woods.

"Please execute a U-turn and return to the nearest road," requested the navigation app.

"Easy for you to say!"

She took advantage of a precious moment, during which the path immediately in front of the van didn't present the looming threat of collision, to look at the scrolling map on her screen. It was mostly green, but off to the northeast was a narrow gray stretch with the unmistakable easy curve of a man-made road.

"We'll head that way. The stupid road's got to lead *somewhere*, right?"

The van's bumper got a good workout as she plowed through bushes, then another impromptu flight signaled her departure from the forest and her arrival on what turned out to be an old logging road. She landed hard and straightened the vehicle out.

"In one thousand feet, turn left," the GPS instructed.

"Now you're talking!"

Following the directions offered up by the navigation required a few more questionable acts, including bursting through a chained gate, but eventually she spilled onto a back road only a few turns away from a major highway. The van wasn't exactly untouched from the ordeal. She was down to one headlight, the front driver's side tire seemed a bit wobbly, and about half of a Douglas fir was dragging behind her, but she was still moving, and the police were nowhere to be seen.

She straightened her glasses and took a breath.

"There… that wasn't so bad…"

***

Despite his better judgment, and the fact that his brain was badly in need of sleep, Markus had relented to Blodgette's gentle insistence that she take another late-night dip.

"I'm hoping we can get your language skills developed soon, so I can explain to you why standing out here in the middle of the night when we *know* there are wolves around is a *terrible idea*," he said.

The night had gotten downright icy, but if it bothered Blodgette, she didn't let on. He, on the other hand, had wrapped himself in an emergency blanket he'd found in a back room. While he was at it, he'd bandaged up his scalded hand.

"We're going to have to see if we can work out a schedule for this sort of thing. Or at least get Gale to give me the lowdown on what temperature you're supposed to be at when it's bath time. Something tells me you're taking advantage of my ignorance to get some bonus lake time."

He raised his head and spotted a single headlight. A shock of fear stung his stomach, then a distracting realization that the fear of a human being discovering him was more frightening than another wolf encounter. He was still grappling with this worrisome realization when the puttering van limped into the courtyard.

"I'm back!" called Gale. "The guard wasn't even there. He left the gate open, can you believe it? Best forty bucks I ever spent! … Something wrong?"

Markus stared at the sorry state of the van. "What happened?" he said.

"To the van?" she said.

"Yeah, to the van! You're dragging a forest behind you."

She popped the door open and hopped out. "Wow, I *am* dragging a lot. So *that's* what that sound was. Anyway, don't worry about it. I handled it."

"Be that as it may, what is it that you handled?"

"There was a run-in. How's Blodgette doing?"

"She's fine. What run-in?"

"With the police, but no problem. It's taken care of."

"You had a run-in with the police!"

"It was nothing, really!" Gale said.

She tried to tug open the back door of the van and found it badly buckled. A few more vigorous pulls caused the whole door to drop off its hinges.

"That seems like a hell of a lot more than nothing."

"Look, they saw me, they chased me, but I lost them, and then it was clear sailing all the way here. Boy, it got kind of shaken up back here. Lucky I packed the way I did."

She grabbed one of the potted plants, which had been evicted from its pot during the ride.

"They chased you?! You got into a police chase?!"

"It was taken care of. I'm no dummy. Look, see?"

She pointed to the license plate. "Covered up. No license plate, no connection to you or your uncle or anything."

"No connection to… *look at the side of the van, Gale!* Dimitrios's Deluxe Delivery. With an address and a phone number!"

"Oh… yeah… I forgot about that…"

"How could you forget about that?!"

"I panicked! It was my first high-speed chase, okay? But I think we're still good. They definitely didn't follow me, and the roads were *empty* on the way here. We've got time."

"Do we have two years? Because that's what it's going to take, right? That's how long we're going to have to stay ahead of the law if we're going to get Blodgette off to a good start, right?" He shook his head. "She is so screwed. We totally screwed up…"

"We'll figure it out. Don't worry," Gale said, putting her hand on his shoulder. "Can I… can I make an observation?"

"Does it involve any more revelations about major agencies that are going to be after me?"

"No. Well, yeah, actually. Animal Control. But that's not what I was going to say."

"What then?"

"I'm happy to see at some point between when I left and now this became about Blodgette growing up right instead of you avoiding jail. Did something happen?"

"No... Actually... she..." Panic and frustration flickered briefly to embarrassment. "She called me Mom."

"She *called* you Mom? How?" Gale said, any semblance of concern about the police washed away by the revelation.

"She spelled it out. We were playing with building blocks."

"She's spelling?!"

"I know, it's crazy, right?" he said, the realization re-dawning and bringing a smile to his face.

"That's incredible. We've got to see if she'll do it again when we get back inside. But that's all it took? Three little letters and you're onboard?"

"Hey! I was onboard from the start. But it had a certain heart-melting effect, I'm not going to lie. And speaking of melting, I think I figured out how she keeps her temperature in check better than the rest," he said, holding up his hand.

"Oh no! Did you burn yourself? The *Structophis gastrignae* shouldn't have any dangerous temperatures externally at this age."

"Those horns of hers are *rocket* hot."

"They are?" She slapped her head. "Of *course* they are. Like a heat sink! She's got naturally occurring heat sinks!"

She turned to the lake. Blodgette, satisfied with her dip, was trudging up the slope. She had a measured expression on her face, as if she was happy to see that Gale had returned, but not so happy that she'd want Gale to *know* she was happy. Once she spotted the flower in Gale's hand, the attempt at concealing her happiness toppled and she made eager grabbing motions.

"Yeah, this is for you!" Gale said, handing it over. "You're a *special* one, aren't you? I swear, Markus, I've been reading up on these things for years and I've never heard anything like this happening before. I don't know if this is a beneficial mutation—*Structophis gastrignae* are known for their genetic malleability—or if it was a purposeful physical modification. There *have* been documented examples of creatures modifying their bodies all the way into adulthood, but normally it's to facilitate their chosen fixation. This could have been a survival adaptation to take care of the poor choice of oven. There's the off chance we'll be able to ask her, if she gets her head around the language fast enough. But only if we don't get caught..." She sagged a bit. "Which isn't too likely now. ... We *did* screw this up, didn't we?"

The realization of the consequences on not just one but three lives swept in and weighed down upon them. Blodgette stopped sniffing at the flowers long enough to realize the somber tone that had seized the rest of the group. Though still dripping with water, she decided all of this sadness was entirely unacceptable. She plodded up between them and squeezed them both into one big, wet hug.

"Yes, Blodgette. Thank you, Blodgette," Markus said, trying to shove her away before he was completely soaked.

"She's hugging me! She's hugging me too!" Gale proclaimed. *"I've been accepted into the family group! WE'RE PACK BONDING!"*

The escalating excitement was enough to convince Blodgette to let her go and look warily at her.

"I've got to write this down! Oh my gosh, I feel like Jane Goodall!"

Blodgette looked to Markus. He shrugged.

"She means well. Come on. Let's go see what else she got for us and get it inside."

***

The following morning, Dimitrios and Grumman arrived via a nondescript rental car at the bistro. A police car was parked out front, and one of the officers was standing guard in front of the door.

"What seems to be the problem, officer?" Dimitrios asked, springing spryly from the passenger door of the car.

"This place of business is under investigation," said the policeman.

"I can see that," Dimitrios said. He fished out his wallet. "My name is Dimitrios Spiros. I'm the owner of this bistro."

The police checked his credentials, then turned to Ms. Grumman. "And you?"

She presented a gold-embossed business card. "Ms. Grumman. Your superiors should have been provided information about me and my role in this investigation."

"Oh, right, right. You're the... what's the word the boss used...?"

"Special envoy. I am to be treated as a consultant with full privileges." She checked her phone. "If I have been properly informed, this investigation is regarding a recent incident farther north."

"Yeah. Some crazy chick pulled some seriously reckless driving in some Podunk burg. Big, clunky grease truck, and yet somehow the county cops up there couldn't chase it down. Had this place printed on the side. At first we assumed it was just stolen, but the old biddy upstairs says it was taken by the son of the owner."

"Nephew," Dimitrios and Grumman corrected simultaneously.

"Whatever. We took a look inside and, hoo boy, *something* went down in there. Busted-up woodwork. Water all over the floor. It was a... *hey! Hey! What'd I tell you?!*"

The policeman had directed his outburst at a trio of men in black slacks and black dress shirts who were approaching from down the street.

"*These* guys. When we got here, they were snooping around. Wouldn't answer *any* questions about why they were here, what they were doing. They're lucky I didn't haul them in! Number one suspects right here."

"As a matter of fact, Officer, these gentlemen represent a private security firm hired by Herr Spiros. They had permission to investigate the premises. Including all rooms currently inaccessible." She turned to Dimitrios. "Isn't that correct, Herr Spiros?"

"Hmm? Oh, yes. Yes. Private security. Yes. Must protect my property, after all," Dimitrios replied, slow to catch on.

Ms. Grumman pulled a briefcase from the car and withdrew several very official-looking documents.

"Everything should be in order," Grumman said.

The officer looked over the files, visibly confused by the wording. "I'm going to have to run this by the pencil pushers in the department."

"By all means. Any proper law enforcement officer must do his due diligence to ensure there have been no improprieties."

He stepped aside and pulled a radio from his belt.

"Herr Spiros, if you would, please stand by to answer any questions about the property that the police might have. I need to debrief your security."

"Fine, fine," Dimitrios said. "You've got to keep an eye on the police anyway. Can't tell you the trouble these boys have caused me thanks to the lady upstairs, who moved into the apartment over a bistro knowing full well it would be noisy and yet suddenly that becomes *my* problem. Some people…"

He continued his rant, to no one in particular, and wandered over to the policeman. Ms. Grumman approached the black-clad lurkers.

"Have you been updated on the current state of affairs?" she asked.

"Vehicle sighting during a police incident a few hundred miles north of here," said the tallest of the crew.

"Indeed. And scattered reports of a similar vehicle driving erratically on the freeway, tracing a line north to approximately the site of the police incident," she added. "No confirmation of the target cargo, but I am confident we can act as though the vehicle contained our target. Perhaps not at the time of the primary incident, but certainly during the preceding trip. If we operate under the assumption that Markus Spiros and Gale Dekker stowed the target prior to returning to the rest stop, that gives us a search radius of anything within a forty-five minute drive of the rest stop. I've got people in the home office researching places within that radius that suit the target's maintenance needs. Unfortunately, it is an extremely rural area. With planning, any section of it could be rendered a proper location for storing the creature without observation."

"A grid search may be necessary," he said.

"Something that will waste precious time and open us up to discovery," she said. "I believe…"

An obnoxious ringtone managed to short-circuit even *her* steel trap of a mind. She glared in Dimitrios's direction and watched as he pulled out a phone and answered.

"I'm in the middle of something, can I… Oh, Beeni! It's you. *No*, I wasn't dead. I was in Europe. … Yes. Business. … Yeah, I remember Markus. To tell you the truth, I've been looking for him. … Yes, I figured you sent him down here. Damn good thing you did, too. You wouldn't happen to know where he went, do you? … Markus. … Yes, I remember him, Beeni, we were just talking about him." He covered the microphone. "She's down to about half her marbles."

Ms. Grumman stepped up to him. "Herr Spiros, is that Sabina Templeton with whom you are speaking?"

"Yes. My niece. I… just a second." He raised his voice. "Yes, Beeni, I remember Markus."

"She is the last person to speak to Markus. I wonder if you would allow me to have a word with her."

"You can try," he said. "Beeni! Listen. Listen, there's a lady here. Business associate. Wants to talk to you. … Ms. Grumman. … No, that's Phyllis, Bobby's girl. You haven't met this one. No, she's not a friend of Markus's. … Yes, I remember Markus. Look, just talk to her for a bit."

He handed the phone to Grumman with a good-riddance gesture, then set about bothering the police officer again.

"Hello, Frau Templeton."

"Is this Phyllis?" asked the voice over the phone.

"No, Frau Templeton. This is Ms. Grumman. I am presently working with Herr Dimitrios Spiros."

"Oh, yes! Dimitrios. Have you met Dimitrios?"

"As I just finished saying, Frau Templeton, we are temporarily aligned in our business dealings. You are a difficult person to contact. We have been calling quite steadily."

"Oh, I don't answer any phone calls from numbers I don't know. Same goes for the door. *Everyone* is trying to sell you something. Everyone's got their own scam. Oh, confidentially, you know who is *always* running a scam. My Uncle Dimitrios. Have you—"

"*I have*," Grumman snapped, briefly losing her composure. She took a breath and continued. "I would like to ask you a few questions about Markus."

"Oh, yes. He's my nephew. Dimitrios's great nephew."

"Yes. I presume you have already been asked, quite extensively, where he might be found."

"Just by Uncle Dimitrios. Have—"

Ms. Grumman quickly spoke to cut off the inevitable restart to the conversation. "I further presume he did not *tell* you where he went prior to his departure."

"No, no. All I know is he went down to the bistro. I only talked to him once more after that."

"I see. And what was that final conversation regarding?"

"He wanted to know about that nice summer camp he used to go to. Did you know they turned it into a nature preserve?"

"I believe the term is 'nature *reserve*,' Frau Templeton. And I am afraid I do not know the camp to which you are referring."

"Such a nice place. So many kids learned so much about nature. Now they've taken the kids out and just let the *nature* take over. Seems kind of pointless if you ask me. Though my nephew Markus would still love it. Do you know Markus? He's my nephew. He's *very* interested in animals."

"Delightful, Frau Templeton. If you could provide me with the name and/or address."

It took seven more introductions to either Dimitrios or Markus, but eventually she was able to get the name of the former camp. With the information in hand, she quickly foisted the phone back onto Dimitrios and pushed the information to her staff. In moments they returned the relevant summary. She allowed herself a fraction of a degree of an upward shift at one corner of her mouth that counted as a smile for her, then addressed the leader of the "security team."

"This is the place. Most assuredly. A large body of water, access to minerals, and secluded. It is perfect," she said.

"Should I get the team up there?"

"Not just yet." She looked over her shoulder to Dimitrios.

"... No, it was *Italy* I was visiting. ... By the way, did you know that *that's* where mozzarella comes from? ... No, not Germany at all..."

She turned back, comfortable that he was far too distracted to overhear her.

"The individual presently in possession of the target may not be willing to part with it. It is thus prudent to produce some leverage to help us persuade him, or failing that, to provide the first breadcrumb that will lead authorities to our desired conclusions about him. I assume you have kept the police under close surveillance?"

"As instructed."

"And has their search been thorough?"

"They are operating with a limited search warrant. They cannot access any of the storage areas not already damaged."

"Excellent." She pulled a small slip of paper from her pocket. "Following their departure, which I shall see to it is as expedient as possible, have one of your team enter the building and place any two of the items from this list in one of the un-searched storage areas."

"Acknowledged."

"Excellent."

She turned and approached Dimitrios and the police officer.

"Officer, I have spoken with Herr Spiros's security, and combined with your no doubt thorough work, I believe we are satisfied with the results of the investigation. We would prefer if you left the premises immediately."

"Whoa, whoa, whoa, lady. I only *just* finished confirming you're even allowed to *be* here. And you might have some sort of clout, but I've still got a job to do, and I've still got my orders. I'm not going anywhere until *I'm* satisfied."

"I see. If you'll pardon me for a moment."

She pulled her phone from her pocket and tapped a contact number. "... Yes, this is Ms. Grumman. I am having some difficulty with local law enforcement outside the bistro. They are refusing to leave the investigation to Herr Spiros's private security. ... Of course."

Grumman held out the phone to the police officer. "It is the senator's office. I believe you have new orders."

The officer gritted his teeth and took the phone.

Ms. Grumman took Dimitrios aside. "At the conclusion of this phone call, the officer will reluctantly remove his men from the bistro, but he is still within his rights to take a statement from you, and he will quite rightly demand to do so. You shall tell him the following. Markus Spiros is a former employee and family member. He has had access to both the bistro and its delivery vehicle, with your permission, for quite some time as a favor unrelated to the operation of your business. He has been visiting after hours with escalating frequency in the last seven months, and while this is not the first time he has borrowed the catering truck, this is the first time he has not returned it prior to start of business the following day."

"That's not exactly true. He hasn't been to the bistro in five years."

"I am aware of that, Herr Spiros. But when asked, you will give the information I have provided."

"It seems to me you want me to tell an awful lot of lies to the cops. That's putting me in a tight spot, isn't it? Why should I take all of this risk?"

"Because you have been paid fifteen million dollars for your compliance, and noncompliance at any point until the successful acquisition will forfeit the remaining fifteen million."

"Oh, right! The *rest* of the money. Okay, so *how* often has Markus been visiting...?"

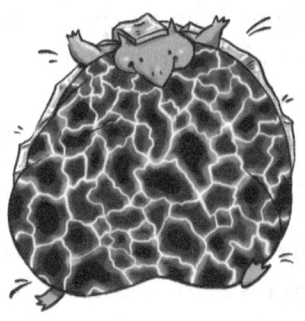

Chapter 8

Three hours later, Markus groggily opened his eyes. He'd been sleeping fitfully. It turned out Blodgette was a heavy, *heavy* sleeper. She snored quite a bit, which would have been loud enough by itself, but since she was outfitted with what amounted to a suit of armor, each heavy inhale rattled her plates like someone trying to open a stuck junk drawer. It wouldn't have been so bad if she'd curled up in her own room, but she was sprawled out next to Markus, near enough that the very real risk of her rolling on top of him kept him on edge. He'd tried to move discreetly to another room twice over the course of the night, but each time Blodgette had eventually woken up and groggily found him before flopping down beside him again.

Once sunlight started shining through the windows, he gave up on trying to sleep and shuffled into the hallway. Two rooms away, the clicking of keys drew his attention. He poked his head into a room with a conference table and found Gale seated at it, hammering away at a laptop.

"Oh, you're up! Good, I had some questions to ask you," she said, shuffling through a list of handwritten notes.

"Don't you ever sleep?" he asked.

"Sleep? At a time like this? No, sir."

"But… it's a physical need…"

She dug into a bag beside her and tossed him a petite black can.

"Cold-brewed coffee shots. These babies are what got me through the last three exam sessions. Highest caffeine content this side of those trucker pills they used to sell. There's actually a recommended daily maximum for that stuff, but take it from me, it's *way* conservative." She found the note. "Okay, so would you say you have a genuine interest in Blodgette's welfare?"

"Of course."

"Would you say you are physically able to fulfill your responsibilities regarding her care?"

"So far, at least."

"Do you have *time* to fulfill those responsibilities?"

"Considering I'll probably be fired if I miss another shift, yeah, I'd say my schedule's open."

She looked to the page. "You don't have any children. ... The money to raise her is still a question mark... Do you feel you are morally equipped to produce an upstanding member of society?"

"I guess so. What's this about?"

"There's no reception and thus no internet in this place. But while I was on the road I pulled down some wiki pages and a bunch of stuff from legal forums. The law, as it applies to *Structophis gastrignae*, is a little fuzzy. They're teetering on the legal definition of 'person.' Or, more accurately, 'citizen.' I'm thinking we've got a pretty good chance, if we get the right lawyer, to make you Blodgette's legal guardian. You fulfill most of the criteria, and if Blodgette is declared your ward, or even a ward of the state, then she's no longer contraband or a mistreated animal or any of the other illegal headings she might fall under that could get you locked up. There'd be a potentially *new* hornet's nest of child endangerment and stuff, but it's all such a blurry line that the lawyers could probably duke it out for well over the two years it'll take for her to 'leave the nest' so to speak."

"Legal guardian. Like... like I'd adopt her?"

"If we can get her under the legal heading of 'child,' yes! Absolutely. It's a great idea, if you ask me. And I mean, she already calls you Mom."

He leaned against a wall.

"The weight of it still hitting you?"

"It comes in waves," he said.

A chirp came from the other room, then the distinctive sound of several hundred pounds of pizza dragon pulling itself to its feet. She lumbered through the hallway, chirping curiously until she spotted him, then thumped over and grabbed his hand. She tugged him toward the hallway and pointed to one of the doors with a quiet burble.

"I think it's time for a feeding," he said.

"Or she wants to take a swim."

"No, when she wants a swim it's more of a high-pitch thing."

"Really?" she scribbled it down. "See? You're already picking up on her vocalizations."

They made their way outside, where Blodgette eagerly grabbed some firewood from beside the door and gnawed on it.

"There're basically two big problems to solve. The first is any of the legal problems. Whether she's a child or an animal, if doctors decide she's been mistreated and find you culpable, we're in trouble. That's why *this* is important." She pulled out her thermometers. "Temperature time!"

Blodgette worked her way through the poses necessary to take the various temperatures. The only thing she refused was the temperature in her mouth, which was otherwise occupied with her kiln-dried hardwood breakfast.

"She's *very* stable. I think we can make the argument that she's had *very* few physical consequences. That just leaves the money. And *this* should take care of that."

She slipped a folded piece of paper from her back pocket and handed it to him. He opened it and read the words scribbled on it.

"'The Marvin C. Wintergarten Endowment for the Advancement of Natural Sciences,'" he said.

"It's perfect," she said. "It's a *massive* endowment, and they don't give it out every year. It only goes to research projects," she tapped the page and quoted it, "'that go above and beyond in their pursuit of unique insight into the natural world in areas otherwise inaccessible to scientific investigation.' I *challenge* you to find someone who has gone further above and beyond in the pursuit of something as unique as this. A single human, raising a *Structophis gastrignae* as his own child for the duration of its intellectual development? It's unprecedented! And that endowment is for $875,000 per year for the duration of the study, if selected. That's *more* than enough to support you, support Blodgette, and as a nice bonus, carry me straight through to my doctorate."

He nodded, reading over the rest of the notes on the page. "It *does* sound as if it would be just the ticket, but I see you've got something written here, and it's underlined twice with a frowny face next to it."

"Uh... Yeah. *Technically* any laws broken in the process of the scientific study are grounds for immediate disqualification for the endowment. But if we can work out that guardianship thing, no problem."

He rubbed his forehead. "I'm detecting a loop here. If I can get the money, I can become her guardian; and if I can become her guardian, I can get the money. You've put together a nice little Catch-22."

"Pick, pick, pick," she said, snatching the page away. "You call it a problem, I call it ninety percent of a solution. That we can get this close means there's hope. So quit moping and get to parenting. All the literature says that *Structophis gastrignae* develop into happier and better-adjusted adults if they are kept constantly stimulated during this stage of their development. Usually there're at least one parent and an entire community to do the job, but right now there're just you and I, so we're going to have to work a little overtime."

Markus scratched his head. "Education. So what should I be working on?"

"There's been very little research put into seeing how *Structophis gastrignae* tackle math. Maybe give that a try."

"Yeah, okay," he said, looking around.

He paced across the courtyard to the shore of the lake. Blodgette watched him go for the first dozen steps, then decided

he was getting entirely too far away. Since snack time wasn't nearly over, she awkwardly grabbed some wood under her arm, then
handed a few logs to Gale and thumped out to where Markus
had begun to collect rocks. When she arrived, he'd collected a
dozen or so similar-size stones and cleared a patch of ground.

Blodgette must have been catching on to when she was about
to get a lesson, because she obligingly took a seat and watched
with interest as Markus started arranging the stones.

"Okay, Blodgette. This is one." He separated a single stone
from the rest. "And this is two." In a similar manner, he illustrated the rest of the numbers through ten.

"I'm not sure this is the best way to start with math," Gale
said, briefly attempting to take notes while still holding the rest
of Blodgette's snack. Once she realized she didn't need to be carrying the wood anymore, she dropped it and scribbled out notes
more efficiently. "She doesn't look engaged. She's very distracted,"
she said.

Markus glared at her. "Maybe that's because there's a hyperactive grad student taking notes and picking nits, which, like
most things in the universe, is more interesting than learning
arithmetic."

"Fine, fine. I'll give you some room."

She backed away, nearly tripping twice rather than sparing
more than a fleeting glance away from her notebook.

"Here's the tricky part, Blodgette. Listen up. This is two. And
this is three." He illustrated each with arrangements of stones.
"And if you put two and three together, you get five." He made a
third pile. "See? This, plus this, is this."

Blodgette crunched down the rest of her current snack, released a sooty belch, and leaned down to investigate the piles of
stones. She jabbed a finger at the first pile and chirped, then the
second with another chirp, and finally poked at the last. A few
doubtful glances and warbles of disbelief suggested she was not
convinced of his assessment.

"I assure you, I'm not the best at math, but this I can do. There're five stones here, and then one, two, three, and then four, five."

She shook her head and crossed her arms, now quite certain he didn't know what he was talking about.

"You've got to assert authority and confidence or she'll never learn," Gale called.

"Stop being a backseat parent! I'm doing this!" he called back with irritation. "Here, Blodgette. I'll show you. See? Watch."

He moved the stones around, positioning the two stones with the three stones until they matched the arrangement of five.

Blodgette blinked and pointed, trilling with surprise and clapping. He may as well have done a magic trick, turning something that was *not* five stones into something that definitely *was* five stones.

"See? *Told* you I knew what I was talking about," he said. "Now let's try another one."

For ten minutes Markus worked his way through a handful of simple addition problems. The dragon watched like a child at a puppet show, bouncing and twittering with excitement every time he illustrated the answer.

"I don't think she's actually learning. I think she's just being entertained," Gale called again.

"Do *you* want to do this?" Markus said.

"Yes!" she said.

She marched over and handed him the pad.

"Write down anything notable she does," Gale said. "You see, you don't start with addition and subtraction. Early learning, particularly with animal intelligence, is supposed to focus on comparison. Greater than and less than. It's the simplest inroad to mathematics, because the mind of a living creature is designed around the concept of seeking more, so she should already have an instinctive understanding."

She took three of the remaining bits of firewood and arranged them in front of Blodgette, one stack of two, and one by itself.

"Which one is greater, Blodgette?" she said loudly and slowly. "Take from the one that has *more*."

Gale turned to Markus. "See, first you teach her that some numbers are larger than others, *then* you start getting into absolute value and all that."

She turned back and watched Blodgette expectantly. Blodgette stared back at her, blinking now and then and waiting. The dragon had the same posture and expression of someone watching an unfamiliar comedian and was growing weary waiting for the punch line.

"Which one is *more?*" Gale repeated.

Blodgette huffed a sigh, then reached out and gently gripped Gale's shoulders, guided her out of the way, and pointed to Markus, then to his piles of stones.

"Hold on. I've got to write this down. 'Gale... failed... mis-er-ab-ly.'"

"Oh, ha ha," she said, marching up and snatching the book. "The joke's on *you*, because finding out what does and does not work for education is absolutely the sort of thing I'm trying to learn. So this is a successful experiment. But let's see you do better."

Markus stepped up, and immediately Blodgette's disposition brightened and she became more interested. Again he arranged stones, this time two and three again.

"Here we go. Show me how many is two plus three," he said.

Blodgette looked at the two piles, then looked to the empty spot beside them and pointed expectantly.

"No, *you* fill that in. *You* show me how many go there."

She twisted her head, then looked down again, face screwed up in deep contemplation. She selected a stone from the pile of spares and hovered it over the empty area awaiting a solution. She paused for a few seconds without dropping it. Suddenly Markus could practically *see* the lightbulb light up over her head. She tossed the stone back where it came from, then reached down and gathered the piles of two and three, brushing them together into one pile, then sliding the pile over to the "answer" spot. When she was through, she pointed and chirped.

Markus considered this. She'd arranged the correct answer, in the correct spot, and didn't do any math to do it.

"Honestly, Blodgette? I think you might be smarter than both of us," he said appreciatively.

She held up a hand expectantly.

"Heck yeah, high-five," Markus said, obliging her. "But let's see if we can get the right answer the hard way."

Blodgette clapped and watched excitedly as Markus arranged a new problem.

"Got any commentary, Ms. Documentarian?" Markus asked.

"I'm not sure if it's educational, but it's definitely enrichment. Keep it up, this is good stuff!"

"Happy to oblige," he said.

As he went to work, his belly rumbled. This brought the lesson to a sudden and immediate end as Blodgette completely disregarded any attempted arithmetic and chirped in concern. She grabbed one of her precious hunks of wood and handed it to him, patting his stomach.

"Yeah, uh. Though it may be breakfast time, this isn't going to cut it for me. Don't worry about it, I'll get something to eat after—okay then, I guess we're going."

Blodgette had heaved herself to her feet and grabbed his hand, tugging him along back toward the building. Gale followed after them, scribbling eagerly on the pad.

"I've never seen anything like it. *Powerful* maternal instincts at an age while she is still dependent on her own parents. Fascinating…"

***

A police car cruised slowly along a gravel road in the mountains nearby. Ever since Gale's rather absurd and unlikely escape, he had been weaving through the local service roads looking for some indication of where the truck had gone.

"Seems like an awful lot of trouble for reckless driving, Jonesy," remarked the man in the passenger seat, Officer Henderson.

"Do you have something better to do, Henderson?" he said.

"No, sir, but it was just some crazy kid in a lunch wagon. She's bound to turn up again."

"If you set aside that we've specifically been dispatched to find her, the facts are that the state's pretty darn hot on this one. All points, all that. So it'd look pretty good for any department that turns it up, or more to the point, it'd be pretty bad for a department that lets it get away."

"Even so, Jonesy, the truck *itself* obviously isn't around here. So what do you think we'll find?"

Jones squinted along the side of the road, then pulled over. "What's that right up there, Henderson?" he said, pointing to a shiny piece of metal by the side of the road.

Henderson popped the door and hauled himself out. He knelt beside the bit of debris and brushed it off, then picked it up. "Looks like a passenger-side mirror, Jonesy. From the looks of it, it ain't been here long."

"Well then that's just what we've been looking for. Bring it here."

Henderson brought it over and the pair investigated.

"Definitely commercial. Just the sort that'd be on a catering truck." Jones grabbed the radio. "Dispatch, we've got a possible piece of debris from that bistro truck we're after. We're back on Sawmill Road 4. Seems to me a truck like that isn't going to get far on mountain roads like this. What're the closest pieces of property with maintained roads?"

"Let's see... There're a few."

"Well put together a list. And get Rimly and Buck in their gear and out to Sawmill while you're at it. If the state's after that truck, we could probably use the backup."

"Roger, Officer Jones."

Jones hung up the radio microphone and grinned. "Nice thing about a small town, Henderson—there are never too many places to look."

***

Blodgette was just finishing up her afternoon dip as Markus stood at the edge of the courtyard, poking at a grill. It was covered with chicken breasts and hamburger patties.

"You know something," he said. "This is bringing back some good memories."

"Is it?" Gale said, distracted as she looked over Blodgette's chest armor.

"Sure. Every summer, while I was at the camp, we'd have barbecues right here on this grill. It was movie night, too. They'd set up a screen over there and we'd watch cheesy family movies. Good times."

Blodgette moseyed up to Markus, sniffed curiously at what he was cooking, then plunged her hand into the bag of charcoal and tossed a handful into her mouth like it was popcorn.

"What are you working on?" Markus asked.

"Look at her chest plate here," Gale said, pointing to a shiny patch. "First off, most of the creatures like her are a combo of doughy flesh and ceramic or masonry, not metal. I would have expected some oxidation or something, what with all the heat and swimming. But she's just as shiny as new. Shinier even."

Gale rubbed a finger across the plates on Blodgette's shoulder. "I think she's sort of keeping them oiled naturally. I wonder if that happens with other creatures, or if this is another survival adaptation thanks to the nonstandard upbringing... And look here. I distinctly remember this being a sort of work-hardened crack in the chest plate when I was first taking pictures."

She snapped another picture, then worked her way backward through the hundreds of photos she'd taken.

"Here, see? Definitely a gap! And now there's just a thin spot, *maybe*. She's *repairing* her covering. That's an *excellent* sign. It not only proves she's getting the nutrients she needs from the stones she's been snacking on, but it means that she's able to grow and change just as in normal development based upon a proper oven."

"So she's going to be fine?" Markus said hopefully.

"It's a *little* early to say for sure she's not going to have further complications, but aside from the outlier temperatures I'm seeing, she's developing perfectly."

He flipped a burger. "That is *fantastic* news. I gotta say, I was really worried about her."

"Sure. Because if she was stunted or otherwise impaired you and/or your uncle would be legally liable."

"No. I mean, well, *yeah*, but no. That's not why I'm relieved. Not by a long shot."

"It seemed to be pretty high on your list of concerns in the beginning."

"In the beginning Blodgette was this big, spooky monster I only remembered in nightmares from the first time she crawled toward me. Now she's... I don't know. She's *Blodgette*. And I'm *Mom* for crying out loud. I mean, what about you? Don't *you* care about her?"

"Of course! I'm studying to be a zoologist. I care about *all* animals, and *Structophis gastrignae* has been my focus since I learned they existed. If I play my cards right, the things I learn about Blodgette and the reports I write about them will be the best thing that ever happened to me, and I'll be able to do *loads* of good for the whole species. Expanding the knowledge of their health and wellness, expanding awareness of the species and its uniqueness. It's a win all around."

"Sure, but I mean, that would have been true if you'd gotten a chance to research any of the pizza dragons. I'm talking about Blodgette specifically as an individual. Heck, as a *person*. Don't tell me you haven't gotten a little attached."

"Sure, she's a sweetheart."

He plopped one of the burgers onto a bun and plated it up. Blodgette, sniffing and investigating a tray of fixings they'd set aside for her, selected a canister of oregano and threw it into her mouth. From the pleasant churr she produced, she quite enjoyed it. After grabbing a second canister, she nosed around the assortment of potted plants that had survived the trip and plucked a vivid purple sprig. She tucked it between two plates of metal near her shoulder as one might stick a boutonniere in a lapel.

"*Oh*, oregano. That's the first herb she's picked out, right?" Gale took the note down. "Fascinating. *Structophis gastrignae* always seem to favor aromatics commonly used in human cooking. Possibly a sign of sort of a symbiotic development? And even the flower. That's jasmine, right? Definitely an edible. I'd like to get my hands on some vanilla. Some exotics, you know? Things that we eat but one isn't likely to find every day. Do they have an instinctive sense for comestibles? Is it something about the essential oils? Fascinating..."

Markus squirted some ketchup onto his burger and spooned on some relish, then plopped down on a folding chair they'd been able to dig up. He took a seat and gazed across the surface of the lake. Something thumped down into the cupholder on the seat. He turned to find Blodgette grinning pleasantly. Either she'd worked out that he had forgotten to grab a beverage before sitting down, or she'd seen a slot in the chair and sought out something to fit into it, since the shaped-pegs-in-shaped-holes toy had quickly become a favorite of hers. If she was simply looking for a round peg, she'd picked something just the right size. If she'd been shooting for a beverage, she clearly hadn't quite learned the difference between her own tastes and those of her caretakers.

"Uh, thanks, Blodgette. I'm sure a can of... Homestyle Tomato Puree would really hit the spot right now, but I think I'll pass," Markus said.

She watched him expectantly for a bit, then made the increasingly familiar chirp of realization and pulled the can from the cupholder. Rather than replace it with something a bit more appropriate, she made a fist and punched the sharp corner of her "gauntlet" into the lid to create an opening for him to drink from. After that, she handed it right back and watched him.

"You *know*," Gale said, tapping her pen on her pad, "*Structophis gastrignae* have been known to take the refusal of their food offerings as a sign of rejection."

"... Yeah?"

Gale nodded. "I'm just saying."

He sighed and braced himself, then took a sip of the canned tomato. Once he muscled the lumpy, cold, and fairly bland substance down his throat, Gale burst into hysterics.

Markus narrowed his eyes. "Let me guess. You made that up."

"Of *course* I made that up. If you turned it down, she'd just pick something else. You weren't kidding though. You've gotten pretty darn dedicated to this parenting thing."

She walked over to hand him a cola to wash the aftertaste from his mouth.

"Thanks. Blodgette, you see this? This is for me, this is for you," he said, illustrating his point about the comparative appropriateness of the two beverages with clear gestures.

The dragon shrugged and grabbed the tomato puree, popping it into her mouth before plopping down on the ground beside him. She stretched her kinked neck out a bit, flopping her head around behind the chair to rest her chin ever so gently on his shoulder. Fresh out of the water as she was, even her particularly hot horns were little more than pleasantly warm.

"Oh, this is just too good," Gale said. She snapped a picture. "I've never read *anything* about *Structophis gastrignae* being so tactile."

Markus reached up and gave Blodgette a little scratch on the chin, prompting a burble of happiness. "You know... let's ignore the questions of how long we'll be able to do this and what sort of consequences it'll have. Right now, in the cool early evening, with a nice burger by the lake... this is kind of nice. I think this is the first time since Beeni first called and started this whole mess that my stomach hasn't been in a cramped-up knot."

"Good! That's good! Animals as smart as Blodgette are *very* empathetic. Anxiety could easily pass right from you to her." Gale turned and squinted in the direction of the road. "And it is for that reason that I'm going to ask you to avoid looking in that direction."

"Why...?" he said nervously.

"No reason," she said, eyes fixed firmly on something in the distance.

Her hopeful charade didn't last for long, as soon the distant wail of sirens shattered the peaceful sounds of nature. Markus stood and looked toward the road. They were only able to make out the merest sliver of road from this vantage, but a police cruiser drifted into and out of view. Markus took a deep breath.

"Okay, Blodgette, we're just going to go inside now. Nothing to worry about. We're certainly not about to be arrested and dragged off to be fined and incarcerated for violating one of several dozen laws and regulations."

The group hurriedly made their way inside.

"Hey," Gale said. "Maybe we'll luck out and they won't be able to get by the guard."

***

"Yes, sure, whatever you say, Officer, uh, Jones!" said the guard, shakily reaching for the gate controls. "I mean, I didn't see anyone come or go, but this is a big reserve, and I'm not here twenty-four seven. Just about anybody could sneak on through. Probably the kind of people who'd tell filthy lies about how they might have gotten inside, just to get decent, law-abiding blue-collar guys like you and me in trouble. Right? Heh. Heh heh. Am I right?"

"Just open the gate," demanded the officer.

"So what's this about, anyway? Some sort of... fugitives?"

"Just. Open. The gate," the officer repeated.

"Right, right." He tapped the control and the gate started to rattle open. "They, uh... they don't give me too much in the way of training. This isn't the sort of thing where you need a warrant or anything, is it? Only because I don't want the higher ups to give me any trouble for violating protocol. I'm all about protocol. Yes, sir. We're nowhere without rules, right?"

The police officer sat down in his cruiser and watched the rickety gate slide open. He made it all of six feet past the gate when his radio crackled with a message from dispatch.

"Car 96, responding to nature reserve. We've got special orders from way up top," instructed the dispatcher.

Officer Jones picked up the radio. "What are the orders, dispatch?"

"There is a special response team on the way, they're about twenty minutes out."

"A special response team?" He peered into his rearview mirror at the police SUV that had accompanied his cruiser, their precinct's closest equivalent to a SWAT team. "*We're* the special response team."

"This is coming from the state office. Seems as though they think this might be part of something bigger."

He grumbled and squinted at the road behind them. "I see three big black vans on the way. No markings. I assume that's who we're waiting for?"

"Yeah. They'll flash some private security badges."

"Private security? We're taking orders from *private security?*"

"No, we're taking our orders from *the state*, and they brought in private security."

"We're sure on the credentials here?"

"I asked all of these questions and got an angry call from Denver that threatened my pension, so leave this one alone."

He gritted his teeth. "Roger, dispatch…"

A road that hadn't seen more that one car at a time in more than a decade was soon crammed with a police cruiser, an SUV, and three large vans with windows conspicuously absent from their cargo sections. The police shifted to allow the vans up to the gate. When they arrived, the side door opened and a severe woman in a crisp business outfit stepped out, flanked by six well-armed individuals.

She surveyed the officers with a critical, distasteful air and addressed them collectively, as though they were the workers of a factory awaiting her instruction on how to operate their machines.

"Ladies and gentlemen," she announced. "As you have no doubt been informed, I am present on orders from the highest level. My team and I shall be the forward-facing individuals for this operation. You all have a very important task to fulfill. We have reason to believe that the individuals presently taking refuge within this facility are engaged in a large-scale criminal enterprise. I have viewed satellite and aerial imagery of the area, and this is the only reasonably maintained road with access to major local byways. If the suspects are to attempt to escape, in any way but on foot through the mountains, this is their only choice of route. For that reason, I require you to withdraw to the intersection with County Road 7, approximately three-quarters of a mile in that direction, and set up a perimeter—"

"Wait, hold on," Officer Jones said. "*This* is the choke point. It's the gate in the fence. A fence is by definition a perimeter. Why the *hell* would we withdraw anywhere?"

She looked at him coldly. "Because you are so ordered by a special representative of your local, state, and federal government," she said.

Ms. Grumman pulled a folded slip of paper from her pocket and presented it to him. He unfolded it. The page was easily the most heavily authorized and authenticated piece of documentation he'd ever held. It was notarized and bore no fewer than three signatures that could end a career and shutter a department.

He cleared his throat and handed it back. "Roger, Ms. Grumman," he said shakily. He slipped into the cruiser and keyed the radio. "Dispatch, units responding to the nature reserve will be redeploying to the intersection of County Road 7 to set up a perimeter."

"Thank you, Officer. The capacity to follow orders is depressingly rare among American police, second only by a tendency to forgo the necessary vetting of authority and credentials. You have demonstrated both skills adequately."

The SUV peeled off and moved down the road to a position with virtually nonexistent sightlines to the former campsite. The armed security piled into the van, but before Ms. Grumman joined them she leaned down to address the officer.

"A final point, Officer," she said. "As you no doubt realize by the individuals from which I draw my present authority, I am entitled to a considerable amount of leeway with regard to how the completion of this operation shall be achieved. I respectfully request your men hold their positions at the perimeter unless extenuating circumstances require your intervention. And in this case, I am comfortable affirming that no circumstances short of direct orders from myself or those listed on my credentials are suitably extenuating. Is that clear?"

"This is your bust. Understood."

"Thank you," she said.

He watched her with unmasked irritation as she stepped into the heavy van and ordered it forward.

"Henderson," he said, addressing his thus far silent partner within the cruiser. "In case anyone ever asks you what a blatant corporate payoff looks like, this is that."

Chapter 9

Dimitrios peered out through the tinted window at the visibly perturbed police officer as he pulled his vehicle back.

"That's very impressive," he said. "Maybe once this is all over, your boss and I could have a word about what sort of steps are necessary for a certain enterprising entrepreneur to get his hands on the kind of piece of paper it takes to boss the police around like that."

"When this is over, Herr Spiros, the single remaining interaction of any kind that you can expect to have with Herr Hearst will be the delivery of the remaining half of your fee, which will be relinquished only with the agreement that you maintain silence regarding the details of the agreement and its results."

"Was that a part of the contract?" he said, scratching his head.

"Am I to believe that you did not thoroughly read through a contract detailing the circumstances and requirements of an eight-figure payout?"

He waved his hand dismissively. "That's all legalese. There's always wiggle room in that stuff. You just let me have a word with him and I'm sure he'll see the sort of value I can add to his firm. Spiros and Hearst, joining forces? That'll be a force to be reckoned with."

"Herr Hearst is already a force to be reckoned with, Herr Spiros. And he has achieved that status by knowing which individuals are worth his continued attention and which are best dealt with and discarded."

Outside Grumman's window, she watched the former summer camp slowly roll into view. "I see a grill. Smoke still rising. Food uneaten. Recent footprints, large and small, in the courtyard. Our targets are here, certainly. Herr Spiros, for the sake of smoothness and simplicity, I would request that you step out first and conduct the opening negotiation. With any luck we can see this through peacefully and swiftly."

"Sure thing, sure thing," Dimitrios said, nodding vigorously. "Negotiation is my specialty." He slid the door open and stepped outside.

Ms. Grumman shut the door behind him and turned to the strike force. "I want you ready to act quickly but only when ordered. The chances of this imbecile successfully bringing the target into our custody are slim, but I will not have so much as a single tranquilizer fired until it becomes absolutely necessary. That said, if it *does* become necessary, I want the assault to be brief and efficient. You are armed with semiautomatic tranquilizer rifles, each with a clip of fifteen experimental tranquilizers. I want extreme shot economy and accounting. Each missed shot will need to be accounted for and cleaned up. Understood?"

The force replied with a single unified nod.

"Excellent. Then all that remains is to watch this fool fail."

**

Dimitrios marched up to the door of the camp's admin building and nearly bashed face-first into it when it, astoundingly, turned out to be braced from the other side.

"Hello?" he said, stepping aside and peering into the windows. "Markus, are you in there? It's me, Great Uncle Dimitrios."

A bit of thumping and rattling followed, then a rustle at one of the windows as a curtain was tugged aside.

"Dimitrios? Where have you *been*?"

"Italy. Long story. Long *profitable* story. I assume you found the, ahem, *item* in the bistro?"

"Yeah, I found her. What were you thinking just leaving her there?!" Markus growled.

"Her? Is it a her now? That's great! Always better to have a female, right? Because of the eggs. Listen, is it... is *she* okay? Hale and healthy? Been taking good care of her?"

"She's fine," he said, his tone distrustful. "Uncle Dimitrios, we saw cops. Why aren't any of them here? And what's with those vans?"

"That? Oh, don't worry. I've got some associates here that'll sweep all this under the rug. Real heavy hitters. But enough about that. I need you to bring 'her' out and we can get this whole thing handled."

"Quit pussyfooting around," barked Gale from farther inside.

She appeared beside Markus and literally tore the curtain down in her eagerness to see the face of the man who'd set this whole mess into motion.

"Do you know the kind of problems you've caused? Do you know how close you came to irreparably injuring the *phenomenally* rare and utterly unique creature we have here? This is a living thing, every bit as intelligent as you or I, and you just left her locked away, *assuming* someone would handle her while you were gone? If *anyone* but Markus had shown up first, you'd already be in jail. And if he'd called *anyone* but me second, both you *and* Markus would be in jail and Blodgette might be *dead*."

Dimitrios blinked at Gale, then looked back to Markus. "Who is this?" he asked, accusingly.

"She's—"

"She's the one who actually knows what's *best* for Blodgette, so if you're going to come marching up here with a bunch of jackbooted *thugs* in big black vans, then you'd better be talking to *me* because if you think I'm going to let you just blow through the three of our lives like a tornado and then walk off scot-free, you have got another thing coming, Mister."

Dimitrios glared at Markus. "You brought a stranger into this? I thought I was clear that this was a private matter."

"*Are you even listening?!*" Gale erupted, rattling the window with her fury.

The escalating exchange evidently had grown too vigorous to ignore, because two ember-like eyes appeared in the darkened room behind Markus and Gale. Blodgette lumbered up to the window and peered out. Her eyes widened and she trilled with excitement at the sight of Dimitrios. Both Gale and Markus objected, but Blodgette was currently beyond the point of listening.

Never one to waste time with things like doorknobs, Blodgette made her grand appearance by pushing the latched front door open amid much splintering of wood and groaning of hinges. She squeezed through the doorway and warbled joyously, throwing her arms around Dimitrios in a hug that, if not for the prior day and night spent calibrating hug pressure in successive experiments with Markus, might have left Dimitrios with a broken rib.

Dimitrios's reaction was an understandable one in the face of the sudden arrival and aggressive affection of a beast the size of a grizzly bear. He froze up entirely, enduring the hug with a startled wheeze. Blodgette released him and grabbed his hand, hauling him inside excitedly.

"Now just one minute!" Dimitrios objected, his objection having roughly the same effect as those of Markus's and Gale's earlier.

Blodgette tugged Dimitrios over to Markus and stood the two men next to each other. She then clutched her hands and released a handful of peeps that had an almost baby-chick level of cuteness. It was clear, without language, that she had finally been reunited with the two most important people in her world.

She threw her arms around the two of them and hugged them tightly, churring happily to herself while Gale dashed to the door and did her best to resecure it.

"I don't recall this level of affection when she first started moving around," Dimitrios groaned.

"She's really come out of her shell in the last day or so. No pun intended," Markus said.

Blodgette chirped and released them, now grabbing each by the hand and warbling like mad as she pulled them through the hallways. Once they'd reached the children's playroom, she led them to chairs and urged them to sit down, then started to rummage through the toy chest.

"What exactly is she doing?" Dimitrios said.

"I think she wants to show you what she's been up to. Uncle Dimitrios, we have to talk about what's been happening. Gale's right. There's a *lot* at stake here."

"You're darn *right* Gale's right!" she said, marching in. "Wildlife endangerment, *child* endangerment, you name it. You're going to have to answer to The Department of Health, and The Division of Family Services, and The Department of Fish and Wildlife, and—"

"Honey, honey, honey, listen," Dimitrios began.

"*Don't you call me 'honey'!*" she fumed. "It's reductive!"

"It's a term of endearment," he said, waving his hand dismissively again.

"It's the chemically altered byproduct of a flower's reproductive process regurgitated by an insect. Who on *earth* thought that was a good idea for a term of endearment?"

Dimitrios raised an eyebrow and glanced at Markus. "Your friend is an odd one."

Before further righteous outrage could be voiced, Blodgette warbled for their attention and then carefully set the picture book on the floor alongside a mound of letter blocks.

"Now what's this about?" Dimitrios asked. "There are some people outside we really ought to avoid keeping waiting."

"Oh no!" Gale commanded. "You sit right there and you watch this. This is the creature you just ditched and left Markus to rescue."

Blodgette flipped through the pages, then carefully matched the images to her guests and started to assemble the letters.

When she was through, there was a row of letters in front of Dimitrios, Gale, and Markus.

Markus gazed down. "Oh, good. I'm still Mom."

Dimitrios had a bit more trouble working his out. "All I see is a mishmash of letters here, what's this? Q-R-V-M-P-A?"

"It's says 'grampa.' She just couldn't find all the right letters. And mine says... I think that's supposed to be a *D* instead of a *B*... DOCTOR!" She hopped up and down, briefly veering from fury to glee. "From your fingers to the degree committee's ears, Blodgette."

Blodgette's chest was so puffed up with pride the metal was creaking. She raised both hands. Markus slapped hands with her. Then Dimitrios found himself the focus of her expectant gaze.

"You've got to high-five her so she knows she did a good job," Markus whispered.

Dimitrios paused, not entirely certain if it was a legitimate instruction, then slowly raised his hand. Blodgette met him halfway and slapped his hand, got her high five from Gale, then burbled happily and started stacking the blocks again.

"Did you train her to do that?" Dimitrios asked.

"This isn't training, Mr. Spiros. This is straight-up learning," Gale said. "You've got to learn that this isn't just some animal, this is a near-human-level intellect that's undergoing rapid psychological development. She's a child and should be treated as such."

Blodgette held up the picture book and pointed enthusiastically at the doctor picture, which, thanks to the presence of large glasses and a clipboard, did indeed have a more-than-passing resemblance to Gale, even if the gender didn't match.

"Yes, that looks just like me," Gale said encouragingly.

"I didn't know they were this smart..." Dimitrios said.

"How did you even end up with one?" Markus asked.

"Mm? Oh. Fellow named Carlos in Italy. Sold me an egg."

"Italy. Sold you an egg..." Gale said, face distant with the effort of remembering.

"Why did you buy one?" Markus asked.

"Come now, Markus. You're my own flesh and blood. Surely you've inherited some of the Spiros Vision. This, er... Bodger, was it?"

"Blodgette."

"Right, this Blodgette was going to be the mascot for the bistro. Well, the delivery end of the business, anyway."

"But it's illegal to *own* one. How were you going to make her a mascot?"

Dimitrios frowned. "Why does everyone get caught up on the little details like that?"

"It's a pretty big detail, Uncle Dimitrios," Marcus said.

"This is one of the abbey eggs!" Gale realized. "The eggs that were stolen from that abbey. They never recovered all of them. They were presumed lost or destroyed!"

"You know about those?" Dimitrios said.

"Of course I know about those. *Structophis gastrignae* is my main area of study, and that theft produced new international legislation imposing massive penalties on the trafficking of these creatures."

"Phew," Dimitrios said. "I'm glad I got in before that went into effect."

"Before that went into effect... Do you think you got grandfathered in on something? *You're still a criminal.*"

"Your friend is very rude," Dimitrios remarked to Markus.

"Listen, Uncle. Let's ignore what happened for a minute and talk about what happens next."

"Right, right. That's *exactly* what I'm here about. I've got it all handled, Markus. Not a problem," he said, switching happily back to the business at hand. "I'll be taking Blodgette here off your hands, and it'll be fine and dandy for everyone. Those people outside are going to take Blodgette and—"

"We're not handing her over to those jackbooted thugs!" Gale said.

"Why does she think there are jackbooted thugs?" Dimitrios asked, once again addressing Markus as though he could act as an interpreter.

"It's a big black van. Who else is going to be in there but jackbooted thugs?" Gale growled.

"Let's hear him out, Gale. We're not exactly spoiled for choice here."

"It's fine. It's all handled, as I said," Dimitrios said. "You see, I sold Blodgette here to those people outside, and—"

"*Sold!* You can't *own* a creature like this, so you certainly can't *sell* one," Gale bellowed.

All of the yelling was beginning to rattle Blodgette, who edged away from Gale and wedged herself between Dimitrios and Markus, holding their hands.

"Who are these people?" Markus asked.

"They work for a fellow named... on second thought, I'm not sure I can tell you. There's lots of paperwork they had me sign, and I'll be honest, I didn't read it. But bigwigs like him usually put in something about not talking about it."

"I don't like this, Markus. Anyone who lawyers up to keep secrets is liable to fall on the evil side of the corporate spectrum," Gale said.

"What are they going to do with Blodgette?" asked Markus.

"That's... not entirely clear," Dimitrios admitted.

Gale was barely able to keep her outrage at a low simmer. "So you're *sure* things will be just fine, but you can't tell us who is going to be taking care of Blodgette, and you didn't even *ask* what they wanted her for?"

"I asked. They just didn't tell me," Dimitrios said.

"And that didn't set off any warning bells for you?!"

"They paid me fifteen million dollars on the spot, and the promise of another fifteen on delivery. When someone offers you that sort of money, young lady, you learn very quickly not to look a gift horse in the mouth."

"Thirty million dollars... We're sure not in 'nonprofit animal refuge' territory, I'll tell you that," Gale said.

"Uncle Dimitrios, if this is going to go down, we need some assurances. We need to make sure that either you or I remain in contact with Blodgette until she's mentally developed enough to be separated, and we need to make sure that she's properly cared for."

He scratched his head. "I think we're past the negotiation phase."

"You're darn right we're past the negotiation phase, because we are *not* negotiating," Gale said. "It's our way or else."

Dimitrios sighed. "Or else *what*, Miss Activist? I really don't think they'll take 'no' for an answer, and they've got plenty of people in that van to make sure things go their way."

"Ah-*ha*! So there *are* jackbooted thugs!" Gale said, stabbing her finger accusingly.

"No, no. Don't be silly. Jackboots go clear up to your knee. These are just the regular work boots. And they look much too expensive to be thugs…"

Markus tried to steady himself, if only for the sake of Blodgette, but the look in his eyes was that of a man realizing that an already maddening situation was spinning even further out of control. He took a step forward.

"Uncle Dimitrios, you and I are going to go out there and"— Blodgette pulled him back and hugged him tightly —"you and *Gale* are going to go out there, and you are going to make it clear, if they want Blodgette, they have to make sure they act in her best interest or they'll have to go through us to get her."

"What exactly is in her best interest? It strikes me I headed to Europe to train up on that stuff and I got a little sidetracked by the outrageous monetary windfall."

Gale eagerly and angrily filled in. "She's got to have the proper environment and nutrition. That means good open spaces to move around in, plenty of seasoned hardwood, moderate amounts of charcoal, plenty of ore. She needs intellectual stimulation, contact with trusted authority figures for guidance, a large body of cool water—"

Dimitrios waved off the torrent of orders. "Just come along. I'll be darned if I'm going to try to remember all that."

"It's not like you'd be able to stop me," Gale muttered.

***

Ms. Grumman stood calmly beside her men. They had stepped out of the van and arrayed themselves around her menacingly.

"Have you got the paraphernalia ready for deployment, in the event our associate proves unable to convince them?" she asked.

"Ready to deploy, as well as the full assortment of low-detection-index accelerants, high-flammability restraints, and the timer," the head of security said.

"Good. I want this clean. Last time we had to pay off the investigators. I don't want a repeat of that."

"Last time you weren't working with the US crew. We're professionals, ma'am."

"We shall see…" She looked wearily to the doorway. Dimitrios and Gale emerged. "Herr Spiros, am I to conclude from the absence of the creature and your nephew that your negotiations have reached an impasse?"

"Not an impasse, as such. Just a hiccup. This young lady is an expert on the beasts. She seems to think she knows what it'll take to keep our investment healthy."

"She's not an investment. And though I'd rather die than see her fall into the hands of a corporation, it's going to take some deep pockets to get her cared for, so if you guys confirm you'll do as I say and *how* I say, I'm willing to consider letting you fund the further care and research."

"My employer is not in the habit of taking orders from outside advisers, nor is he in the habit of having advisers direct his research." Grumman reached into her coat, causing Gale to tense in expectation of a weapon. Instead she removed a silver pen and a black pocket pad. "For the sake of education, what do you believe the creature will require?"

Gale recounted, in exacting detail, every last element of proper *Structophis gastrignae* care. Ms. Grumman silently scratched them on to the page.

"… Markus, possibly Mr. Spiros, and *I* must all have constant and guaranteed contact with the creature to ensure proper emotional development. And finally, I must be permitted to publish my findings on a monthly basis to peer-reviewed journals and for consideration for my degree progress."

Grumman took down this note. "Is that the entirety of your proclamation?"

"Yes."

"Good." She reviewed the list, fetching her phone to compare it to her reference material. "Your assessment closely matches our own. Your knowledge on the issue is to be commended. Would you consider one slight alteration? I believe my employer may be persuaded to satisfy your requirements provided your findings are first cleared by our in-house committee."

"Oh no! Absolutely out of the question. What we learn about this creature, we use to enrich the *world*. And don't even *think* about making promises you don't intend to keep. My brother Donny is a lawyer, and he'll make sure we get all of this in writing and ironclad."

"You are certain?"

"Absolutely certain."

"I see. That is lamentable. As worrisome as the thought of butting heads with *Donny* might be, I am confident the law firms we keep under retainer would be quite capable of solving any issues that might arise. That, however, would produce both delays and publicity, both of which are extremely undesirable at the moment. Permit me to present a counteroffer. We have been in constant contact with state and local police regarding the apparent vandalism of Herr Spiros's bistro and the reckless driving of his delivery van. An investigation is currently on hold at our behest, but when we complete our own investigation, they shall resume theirs. At that time they will discover the following items that we have confirmed to be present in the bistro: approximately seventy-five open boxes of Sudafed. Two hundred unopened boxes of Sudafed. Three containers of—"

"That's a lie! There was nothing *like* that in the bistro."

"This issue isn't what you may or may not have left in the bistro, it is what the police will find there. Now if you will allow me to continue—"

"Listen, I've *seen Breaking Bad*. Sudafed is one of the things they use to make meth. You're trying to frame us as meth dealers? That's crazy! My criminal record is *spotless*."

"There are some animal-control and traffic officials who would beg to differ. But there is still the matter of Miss Tanya Willis, a young lady with an extremely checkered past who fits your description."

"What are you talking about? Who is that?"

"No one. At least, no one currently in the police databases. But new evidence arises so frequently during these special investigations."

"This is blackmail."

"More accurately, this is blackmail with additional coercion, as it is clear your legitimate crimes alone aren't sufficient to motivate you into compliance."

"I dare you! I don't know who you work for, but they're going to be all over the news when I'm done with you!" She turned to Dimitrios. "I'm sorry, Mr. Spiros, but we're going back inside. These people do *not* have Blodgette's best interests at heart."

"*Herr Spiros*," Grumman asserted, "you have received considerable compensation. Do you still intend to do all that you can to ensure the success of this business venture?"

"Sure, but these three aren't making it easy," he said.

"Has the creature illustrated a level of recognition or trust in you?"

"Has it ever," he said, puffing his chest out proudly. "It called me 'Grandpa.' The thing is an awful lot smarter than—"

"That will be all, Herr Spiros. Please stand aside. I am afraid I have been given quite clear instructions. I am to leave with the target in my possession and the secrecy of the situation assured. I mean to follow those instructions to the letter. Gentlemen?"

Gale and Dimitrios looked about, bewildered, as those of Ms. Grumman's team that remained in the courtyard snapped into motion. Some raised their rifles immediately. Others scattered. A shattering thump came from the rear of the main cabin as those who had subtly flanked the group breached the building.

A terrified squeal erupted from Blodgette, unseen within the building, and Markus could be heard trying to calm her. Gale sprinted for the cabin door, but an armed man burst from within and backed her out into the courtyard.

"Hands where we can see them, please," Grumman said wearily. "While I know there is no reception here, and my men have already cut the phone line, I would prefer no attempts at communication or self-defense complicate this any further. Now, inside all of you."

***

Markus fought a breath into his lungs. As threatening as it was to have three heavily armed and armored paramilitary types surrounding him, at this moment the far greater threat was Blodgette herself. She'd been frightened before, but now she was utterly petrified, so much so that she'd forgotten all her hard-earned wisdom regarding the comparative fragility of her squishy caretaker.

"Blodgette, please," he croaked.

She was not in any mood to listen. She trembled, armor rattling and eyes shut tightly. Every inhale was paired with a whistling whimper.

The cramped room slowly filled, first with more hired guns, then with Dimitrios, Gale, and Grumman.

Markus managed to wrestle himself into an angle that permitted more than just a shallow breath every now and then and turned an accusing eye to Dimitrios. "Who the hell have you been working with, Uncle Dimitrios?" he said.

"He seemed perfectly sensible. It's *this* lady that's unhinged," Dimitrios said, eyeing her. "This is precisely why I don't like dealing with subordinates."

"Really, Mr. Spiros," Gale said. "*This* is why? Because they sick jackbooted thugs on you?"

"Enough, all of you," Grumman said. "Though the local police have been given their orders, in my experience the longer they are kept waiting the more likely they are to start sticking their noses where they don't belong. Thus, I shall be brief. Does the creature understand our language?"

"Not so much," Markus said.

"Good, then I can afford to be direct. You look after the well-being of this creature. That is admirable. But your choices from this point forward are limited. There are police waiting to speak to you. This carefully selected hideaway failed to keep you and your ward safe for so much as twenty-four hours. You do not have the capacity to care for or provide for this beast. My employer does. My employer *also* has the resources to make you disappear if you refuse to cooperate. Likewise, any who would search for you or speak in your defense could be easily silenced. Whether you like it or not, these are your last moments with this beast. You can spend them calming it and easing its transition into our able hands, or you can spend them unconscious, courtesy of a rather potent tranquilizer dart. And as trying as your current circumstances are, those you would find yourself in upon awaking would make this moment your last pleasant memory."

Markus took stock of the situation, taking a mental tally of just how heavily outnumbered and outgunned they were.

"What do I have to do?" he said.

Gale fairly exploded at the sound of the words. "You can't just let them—"

Two quick *thwips* of tranquilizers being fired cut her tirade short. She yelped, wavered, and dropped to the ground.

"I am definitely taking a good hard look at that contract when I get home," Dimitrios said. "Seems to me like this is—"

Two more darts found their way into his thigh, and he dropped like a scarecrow.

"One of the few benefits of nonlethal weaponry," Ms. Grumman said, stepping over Dimitrios. "Peace and quiet without the booming report. Now, young Herr Spiros, all you need to do in order to wipe away this entire mess is lead that very valuable creature into the back of our van."

Blodgette shuddered and clutched him tighter.

"Easier said than done. Even if it wasn't being driven by a bloodthirsty corporate villain, Blodgette's developed a bit of a phobia of V-A-Ns."

"Certainly a problem, but when you have solved it, it will be your last. When Blodgette disappears down the road, all your problems go with her. In exchange for this act of cooperation and your continued silence, the evidence of potential drug involvement will mysteriously vanish. Criminal files that could quite easily be linked with you will be conveniently misplaced. Voices with considerable clout will smooth over any rough patches with your education and employment. Your life will return to normal. I trust this is sufficient motivation to get your companion moving in the right direction."

Markus sighed, defeated. "I'll do what I can. Over there in the corner is a sooty old jacket. Bring it over here."

Grumman nodded to one of her men, who obliged. Markus's arms were pinned to his side, so he couldn't take it. Fortunately he didn't have to. During one of her brief, fleeting glimpses to see if the unwanted people had left, Blodgette spotted her much-beloved security blanket in the hands of one of the strangers and chirped angrily. When she reached out and snatched it away, Markus slipped from her grasp and substituted his hand to hold rather than his whole body.

"Blodgette, we're going to go for a walk, okay?" he said.

He attempted to lead her forward, but she wouldn't let him go any farther than her grip would extend, eyeing the surrounding gunmen and holding her ground.

"I'm going to need you to clear a path. At least get out of her eyeline," Markus said.

"Get around behind it," Grumman said. "But keep the guns up."

When the way was clear, and Markus had coaxed for a few seconds, Blodgette grudgingly shuffled toward the hallway. She wouldn't take more than a half step at a time, glancing with fear and bitterness at the others present. When they reached the doorway, she stopped and pointed at Markus's drugged friends and family.

"They'll be fine, Blodgette. They'll be fine. They're sleeping," Markus said.

Blodgette looked doubtfully at Gale and Dimitrios, but resumed her slow, cautious shuffle into the hallway.

"You know, I've been pretty honest with Blodgette so far," he said to Ms. Grumman. "I'd hate to start lying to her now. They *are* going to be okay, right?"

"That depends entirely upon them," Grumman said. "Herr Spiros has proved quite amenable to payment, if perhaps not with the level of understanding one would prefer in a business associate."

"Gale's not going to be as easy to bribe."

"Then Gale will awaken in a few hours in police custody having been implicated in the production and distribution of methamphetamines. She will rave about a ridiculous story of corporate conspiracy and wild animals. A fate you will share if you don't agree to hold your tongue."

He eased Blodgette through another doorway and out toward the courtyard.

"I really wouldn't have thought people like you existed. It all sounds so made up. Paramilitary organizations. Massive payoffs. Poaching of endangered species. I can't believe anyone would do business this way."

"It is the purpose of people like me to ensure that people like you continue to believe that."

Now outdoors, all it took was a single glimpse of the van intended to transport her onward to her uncertain future for Blodgette to lock up again.

"Quickly, Herr Spiros," Grumman said. "If I were you, I would be spending this time illustrating your value to us, and what we value most at the present moment is expedience."

"I'm working on it," Markus said.

His mind worked feverishly, seeking some kind of solution to this problem. Alas, on his best day he was hardly either a world-class schemer or foiler of schemes. Right now he was operating on too little sleep and too much adrenaline. Most of his ideas only got as far as clocking Ms. Grumman on the head and then being perforated with tranquilizer darts.

"Forward, Herr Spiros. Now."

He heard the distinctive clack of a tranquilizer gun readying behind him.

"Look, this is going to sound stupid, but I need flowers."

"Flowers," Grumman said.

"Yeah! She likes flowers! There's a bunch of potted plants over there. Just let me get one."

"Stay where you are." She addressed one of the men. "You. Get one."

The gunman selected a bright yellow flower in a relatively intact pot. This gained the sudden and dedicated interest of Blodgette. Her complex expression suggested she was not only intrigued by the flower, but rather irritated that this stranger was touching it instead of her. She let go of Markus to reach for it.

"Don't give it to her, give it to me," Markus said.

He accepted the pot and stayed a step or two ahead of Blodgette as she quickened her pace to try to catch her two favorite things in the world: Markus and flowers. He made it all the way to the rear bumper before her distaste for large, confining vehicles became the driving factor in her behavior once more. Markus went as far as climbing inside the van himself, but she wouldn't budge.

"Blodgette, listen," he said, stepping back out. "I know half of what I'm saying is gibberish to you, but just try to focus. You've had a hell of a few days. We all have. I know it hasn't been the most pleasant introduction to the world. I wish I could have done better for you, but this caught us all a little off guard. I can't guarantee things are going to work out for us, but you've got to trust me that I'm doing everything I can. You've got to do this. I... I just don't know what else we can do..."

The dragon gazed at him with a degree of understanding. She may not have known what he was saying, but it was clear that she knew it was important, and that something in the speech had made Markus terribly sad and upset. Where the bribes and coaxing and cajoling and threatening had failed to budge her, the look of pain and sadness on Markus's face sparked the maternal instinct in her.

She took one heavy step after the other, each shifting and rocking the van, and climbed inside to wrap her arms around Markus. It wasn't the terrified squeeze of a creature seeking protection. It was the warm hug of someone hoping to offer some comfort. It was a truly heartwarming moment that came to a sudden end with a single word.

"Now," Grumman said.

Acting in unison, gunmen on the left and right sides of the van pulled open doors and stepped inside. Blodgette released a startled peep and tried to back away, but each man secured wall-mounted shackle to her ankles. At first she ignored them, continuing to back toward the rear door. When she reached the end of the chains, she stumbled and reached out to catch herself. This sent Markus face-first into the wall. He dropped to the ground and was promptly pulled from the van as other troopers moved in to affix more chains and deliver a handful of tranquilizer darts to exposed flesh.

Blodgette struggled, then huddled down. As before, in the face of danger she tried her level best to "hide" inside her armor. She squatted down and held her arms, neck, and tail as tightly as possible as her trembling caused the whole van to rattle.

"Get off of me! Get off!" Markus growled, wrestling himself free of the men who'd grabbed him.

They shut and locked the door, prompting a pitiful wail from Blodgette within.

"You can't leave her alone in there!" he said. "She'll have a nervous breakdown! Look at her! Listen, I'll go anywhere you want, I'll do anything you want. Have a goddamn *heart!*"

"The circumstances of my employment place a far greater value on pragmatism than sentiment," Grumman said coldly, fetching her phone. "... Yes, sir. ... Yes, we have the target loaded. ... Yes. ... Herr Spiros, his nephew, and an unrelated third party. No one else. ... Understood."

She ended the call and pocketed the phone. "Well, Herr Spiros, I'm happy to say that my employer has decided to take this opportunity to reduce liability and overhead."

"What does that—"

Thwip.

He felt a hot sting of pain in his thigh, and the world blurred and swayed.

"It means that this is where we say good-bye. With any luck, you won't wake up for the second stage of the plan."

Markus fought mightily to remain conscious, but the large-animal sedative was potent stuff. He hit the ground like a sack of potatoes, the sound of Grumman's voice echoing in his cars as someone dragged him.

"Let's go, people. I want everything in place in five with ignition in twenty..."

***

Gale snorted groggily awake at the sound of a throaty engine roar.

"Huh? Wha...?"

She looked about, but with every motion it felt as though her brain was sloshing in her head. It was impossible to tell how long she'd been out, but however long it had been, the thugs had been busy. Assorted crates were piled on the floor around her, none of which had been present before.

A few moments of sluggish, unsteady lurching finally got her to her feet and she peered inside.

"Clever…" she slurred.

The crates here heaped with assorted drug paraphernalia. Needles, pipes, laboratory equipment… everything one might imagine finding in a meth lab.

"Hello?" she called. "Markus? Dimitur… Dim… other guy?"

Gale took two steps, caught her foot on something soft, and tumbled to the ground again. It turned out the unnoticed obstacle was Dimitrios, still utterly unconscious. She crawled over to him and tried to rouse him, but he was dead to the world.

"See?" she said, shaking her head and instantly regretting it. "If you'd drunk a few cans of that coffee, you'd be up and about too." She used the wall to find her feet again. "Markus? Hello?"

Gale nearly tripped over him as well. They had dumped him unceremoniously on the floor in the entryway. More drug boxes were arrayed around him, but more pressing was the contraption arranged with purposeful precariousness beside a propane tank.

"*Really* clever…"

It was almost a thing of beauty, a plain white emergency candle burning in the center of a nest of torn-up newspaper bunched up around it. The wax had barely begun to run—the thugs must have only lit it a few minutes ago—but left unchecked it would burn down to the paper in less than half an hour.

The crunch of gravel drew her attention to the door, which had been barricaded. In her drugged state, she vaguely remembered hearing an awful lot of banging, but even so, along with the grating that was already on the windows, they'd done a quick job of turning the cabin into the sort of place in which someone would make a last stand against the police.

Through the grated window she could see the van just pulling away.

"Not so fast!" she cried, attempting to tug open the door.

It wouldn't budge. Despite the damage Blodgette had done to it earlier, they'd managed to board it up sufficiently enough that she wasn't going to get it open without a crowbar. That they'd left meant there must have been another door somewhere, but with the lingering effects of the sedative, she doubted she'd find it before the candle trap made the building a lot less hospitable.

She shuffled carefully over to the incendiary threat. While her motor functions remained terribly impaired by the clash of high-octane coffee and animal tranquilizer, she felt her mind was sound enough to defuse the ticking firebomb. This feeling, of course, was the product of a mind currently at the mercy of said biochemical clash, and was only the first of several examples of flawed reasoning that would follow.

Gale at least knew it would be a terrible idea to try to move the candle. It was teetering on the edge of one of the crates and had plenty of newspaper wedged against it, so even getting close was liable to tip it over and prematurely start the blaze. The best idea then was to simply blow the candle out. She crept as near as she dared and took a deep breath.

Once again, if she'd been in her right mind, she might have realized that hyperventilation while feeling light-headed was a terrible idea. She blew once, the puff of air not quite extinguishing the flame. The second deep breath was the killing blow for her equilibrium, and she pitched forward, bashing into the crate and knocking the candle into the paper.

The sight of a mound of newspaper rapidly sparking to flame around a propane tank pumped enough adrenaline into her body to provide her with a moment of clarity. In her impaired state, she had no chance of putting out this fire without getting caught in it. It was spreading rapidly enough to make it clear the newspaper wasn't the only step that had been taken to ensure the spread of the blaze.

Gale did the only thing she could do. She grabbed Markus's legs and dragged him desperately away from the spreading flames.

***

Blodgette couldn't control her shaking. The van was rolling away, and the people who had helped her were behind her, in the building. She was being taken away. Emotions ran high—anger, fear, anxiety—but as strongly as she felt them, she couldn't manage more than a whimper and a shudder when she even thought of trying to do something.

Part of it had to do with the needles they'd shot her with. She looked down to find three still prickling her doughy flesh and brushed them away. They weren't enough to send her to sleep as they had her friends, but they made her feel terribly sluggish and weak.

The van trundled along the uneven road, tipping her from side to side and teetering. She shuffled her feet to catch herself. Something slid and rattled against the wall as she did.

Blodgette looked down and spotted the flowerpot Markus had dropped, with the delivery jacket beside it. She gathered them both up and held them close, sniffing them and trying to detect any hint of Markus's scent. It was there, mixed with the aroma of the flower and the musty scent of the small room that had served as her nursery. Thoughts of that place, and of her rescue from it at the hands of Markus, entered her muddy, tranquilized mind. She took another deep whiff.

This time there was something else, something fresher, more stinging. There was fire somewhere. She raised her nose and found the scent coming from the little vent that blew fresh air into the cramped chamber around her.

"You idiots!" barked Grumman, her voice barely audible through the door that separated her little chamber from the driver's compartment. "I told you we needed at least twenty minutes! The cabin was supposed to ignite while the police were trying to negotiate. It's already gone up in flames."

Only a few of the words filtered through Blodgette's haze of sedative and her weak understanding, but the ones she heard, she didn't like. She raised her head and pawed at the rear door, wishing to see where the scent was coming from.

"We've used this method a dozen times. It is very reliable," her subordinate assured her. "Someone must have woken up."

"Then get this van to the gate, now! I'll get on the radio and see if I can salvage this with the police." After a moment, she continued. "Attention, local police, negotiations have failed. Markus Spiros, Gale Dekker, and Dimitrios Spiros were on-site but had barricaded themselves inside, and it appears they are attempting to burn the facility to destroy the evidence..."

She continued, but the handful of words Blodgette understood rattled in her mind. Markus... Gale... burn...

Fear and anxiety flickered, but the anger surged. Something was happening to her people. Something this terrible woman knew about. As her anger boiled, her temperature began to rise. Chemicals never meant to be put to work on a creature as literally hot-blooded as a pizza dragon sizzled and broke down. Her mind cleared, and with the renewed clarity was a renewed purpose.

There wasn't much room to move in the back of the van, but she was no stranger to cramped spaces. She rocked herself to the side and struck the wall. The van lurched aside and tipped up onto two wheels.

"The beast is awake! Someone get back there and put some more darts in it," Grumman ordered.

Blodgette screeched and rammed herself into the opposite wall. This was the last straw. The whole van tipped over and slammed onto its side, grinding along the gravel. Blodgette tumbled about painfully, her metal armor screeching and clanking against the interior. The collision with the ground wrenched two of her shackles from their mounts, and thus freed, she had the leverage to yank the others free.

One good hard shove tore both rear doors from their hinges, and she crawled from the battered van. Her crusty hide had a few scrapes from the fall, but that was the last thing on her mind. The few minutes of driving had taken her nearly to the opposite side of the lake from the cabin. Great billowing columns of black smoke were roiling out from the structure. The ominous glow of fire flickered in the windows. Grumman and Blodgette clearly weren't the only ones who noticed the blaze, as the police were far closer than Grumman's call would have facilitated.

"Subdue the target!" Grumman cried, crawling through the shattered windshield and flagging down one of the other vans.

The vehicle ahead of them slung gravel as it turned to pursue. The one behind emptied as four gunmen raised their tranquilizer guns and unleashed the ammunition. Needles sparked against Blodgette's armor and punched into her hide, but she was running too hot to even be slowed by the fresh doses. She barreled past the men, whipping her tail at one to launch him into the lake when he tried to physically block her way.

She thundered onward, building speed and momentum. The second intact van pulled up alongside her, and its side door opened. Three gunmen opened fire, thumping additional darts into her flesh with little effect. By now she had more than a dozen of the sedative rounds sticking out of her neck, tail, and thigh. She released a bellow of anger, a deep reverberating sound that pierced the air like a steam whistle. Again she swung her tail, the stout metal spade at the end slashing easily through the driver's side tire. The driver slammed on the brakes and fought to keep control of the vehicle.

Now there was nothing between her and the cabin. It wasn't more than fifty bounding strides away when a deafening thump and ball of flame burst from within. The propane tank had finally blown, rocketing through the roof. Glass burst from the front windows and peppered her, but she didn't lose a step. When she reached the door she dropped her shoulder and bashed through. It cost her most of her momentum, but the blast-damaged door exploded into splinters when she struck it.

Inside, the cabin was utterly engulfed. The propane explosion had damaged the walls and ceiling. Hunks of structure rained down amid violent, crackling flames. Almost immediately she could feel her own temperature rising even more. The anger- and exertion-fueled heat within combined with the broiling temperature of the flames to push her quickly into the danger zone. A different pizza dragon at her age wouldn't have lasted a few minutes at this temperature, but she brushed the danger aside and waded through the flames. Pieces of charred wood bounced off her mask and sprinkled down from above. Part of a wall had collapsed, blocking the main hallway, and the second story seemed ready to come down on top of her. Blodgette almost turned away to seek her friends elsewhere, but behind the wreckage she heard Gale's voice.

"Someone!" she coughed. "There are three people in here!"

Blodgette wrapped her pudgy fingers around the burning wood that blocked the way and heaved it aside. More came down to replace it, but she charged through the tumbling debris and wedged herself through the door behind which she'd heard the voice come from. It was the children's room, where she'd been having her lessons. Separated as it was from the blast in the entry room, it was more intact than the bit of the cabin she'd left behind, but the air was thick with choking black smoke and the flames were threatening.

"*Blodgette!*" Gale said. "Thank god! We've got to get out of here!"

She had the barest sliver of understanding of what Gale said, but the goal was nonetheless clear. The dragon's eyes darted about. She saw both Dimitrios and Markus on the floor. The barred windows were damaged from Gale's attempts to break them out to escape.

All around them the cabin released a worrisome groan. There wasn't much time. Blodgette hefted both Dimitrios and Markus from the floor. Each was still at best semiconscious. Once they were tucked safely under her arms, she paused. She couldn't bring them out the way she'd come in. They would be burned. And the hallway behind was already taking to flame, blocking the only door out of the room. No matter. Doors were more of a nuisance to her than an asset anyway. If she'd learned anything from the last few minutes, it was that for a suitably motivated dragon, anything was a door. She put her tail to work again, hacking and bashing at the wall, trying to break through. It was slow going. The wood gave easily to each chop and bash, but there was a lot of it to go through and not nearly the time to do so.

She turned and put her back to the damaged wall, heaving and throwing her weight against it. Each shove caused more of the wood to splinter and shear, and more of the ceiling to rain down. A final shove tore a Blodgette-size hole in the building and she tumbled out, Gale stumbling after.

As the cool air hit her, it became clear that she was not merely warm, she was dangerously hot. As Gale wavered clumsily after her, Blodgette thumped with purpose toward the lake and dove in. The water sizzled and sang against her flesh and armor. Dimitrios and Markus, already shaken somewhat back to their wits by the jostling journey, were shocked to wakefulness by the unexpected plunge into the icy water. She released them and let them flounder to shore as she completely immersed herself.

She was vaguely aware, during brief returns to the surface for a breath of air, that more and more people and vehicles were arriving at the courtyard, but right now she was far too interested in gulping down her fill of water.

***

Markus coughed and hacked up water as he dragged himself ashore. The tranquilizer, even with the jolt of adrenaline and the impromptu bath, was not quite done with him. He felt sluggish, and his muscles wouldn't quite respond the way he expected them to. Gale, who was better off only in that she had more experience dealing with her disorderly anatomy, helped him unsteadily to his feet, then did the same for Dimitrios.

"What happened?" Markus asked. "What's going on?"

"I don't know. I was out for a lot of it. Are you okay?" Gale asked.

In truth, the whole group had seen better days. Gale was fairly scratched and beaten up. Most glaring was the bruise on her chin from striking the ground when she'd fallen. Markus had a few scratches and burns from the escape. Of the group, Dimitrios had gotten off the easiest, scalded a bit from where he'd been carried by their piping-hot rescuer, but otherwise unscathed.

"I think we'll live." He turned to the cabin, or what was left of it. "Why is the cabin on fire?"

"They tried to burn it down with us in it, that's why," she said.

"Last time I do business with *that* guy..." Dimitrios said, finally reaching his feet and dusting himself off.

"Is Blodgette okay?" Markus asked.

"I don't know. She took a *lot* of heat." She looked around and seemed to become aware for the first time that the police had arrived.

A cruiser skidded to a stop. Officer Henderson in the passenger seat was barking orders and requests for assistance and fire intervention into the radio. Officer Jones threw the door open and put his hand on the grip of his weapon.

"Get down on the ground!" he ordered.

Gale and Markus complied. Their still-impaired equilibrium meant it was a faster trip than they'd intended. Dimitrios refused to oblige.

"I just finished getting up. I'm an old man. And besides I'm a citizen, I know my rights! Take me to your manager!" he babbled.

"Sir, are you currently under the influence?" the officer asked.

"Under the influence of some serious seller's remorse is what I am," he said, wavering. "I never should've sold that thing to that witch's boss." Dimitrios pointed to the approaching Ms. Grumman.

"Officer, you will arrest all three of these individuals," she demanded. "They are involved in drug manufacture, drug sale, drug trafficking, and in the poaching of a rare and endangered animal."

"No, arrest *her*!" Gale countered. "She tried to kill us, tried to frame us for the drug stuff, and tried to *buy* the rare and endangered animal."

"That woman is clearly under the effects of narcotics," Grumman said.

"That's because she shot me with a dart! Look at the thugs! They've still got the tranquilizer guns!" Gale said.

"You've seen my credentials. I will not stand for further delay," Grumman said.

"Everyone listen up," demanded Officer Jones. "I am an officer of the law and I will not be—*holy hell!*"

Motion at the surface of the water revealed something that managed to push the spectacle of a burning cabin to the bottom of the list of priorities.

She emerged from the water like a sea monster. Now that her body, if not her temper, had cooled, she was ready to take care of some unfinished business. The ordeal thus far had left her far worse for wear. The overheated metal of her armor had blued somewhat, and bits of it were already rusting. Patches of her flesh had been baked darker, some approaching black, and here and there bits had flaked off to reveal pale skin underneath. She had the look of a very large, very angry, very overcooked pretzel covered in scrap metal.

Blodgette lumbered up the bank, fury in her expression and purpose in her step. Steam billowed from her mouth and nostrils. Rage smoldered in her eyes. A very uncharacteristic look of fear seized Grumman as Blodgette's oh-so-expressive face made it explicitly clear what she had in mind. Grumman backed away. Blodgette stalked forward. The police did what from their point of view was the only sensible thing. They drew their weapons and made ready to put it down.

"No!" Markus said, climbing gracelessly to his feet despite the guns that were shifting in his direction.

"On the ground!" Jones repeated.

"Don't shoot! That's Blodgette! She's harmless!" Markus said.

Grumman's foot caught on a loose patch of gravel. It unsteadied her sufficiently for the enraged dragon to close in enough to grab the woman by the shirt and hoist her into the air.

"Usually," Markus amended. "She's *usually* harmless."

"Hold your fire. You might hit the woman," Jones instructed.

Markus walked up to Blodgette. "Blodgette! Listen to me! You can't do this. I know what she tried to do. But she failed!

You aren't a dangerous animal, you are a *person*. And people don't kill each other."

Blodgette warbled angrily and pointed at Grumman with her other hand.

"Okay, fine. *Good* people don't kill each other. Prove you're better than her. Prove to the cops and everyone else that you're not a wild animal to be thrown into a cage or a shelter. Let her go."

Blodgette looked at Markus, then glared at Grumman. She held the woman close, face to face. A steamy breath blew Grumman's hair back. Then, as if she were nothing but a piece of trash to be discarded, Blodgette hurled the woman into the lake.

"No harm done!" Markus insisted. "No harm done! She's fine! Everyone's fine!" He turned to Blodgette. "Now listen, I need you to do like this, okay? Like this!"

He slowly lowered himself to the ground as he'd been instructed earlier. Blodgette watched him, then gave the assembled police a critical look. Now that her anger was sated, her natural shyness and anxiety around strangers was creeping back. She took a few steps closer to Markus, watching as the guns followed her, then eased herself down to the ground beside him. Once she was lying in roughly the same way as Markus, she reached over and held his hand.

"Good, Blodgette. Good. Everything's going to be fine." He looked up at the police and the burning cabin. "Sort of..."

***

Three days later, Markus sat in a back room in a courthouse in Denver, Colorado. During the time since the events at the lake, a few things had been made painfully clear to him by a sequence of lawyers, law enforcement personnel, and judges. Despite his good intentions, he had broken a *huge* number of laws. Breaking and entering, destruction of public property, and a dozen minor infractions. The question wasn't if he'd be going to jail, the question was how long he'd be there.

He'd not seen Gale since they'd loaded her into a cruiser to haul her away while she was still reeling from the tail end of her sedatives. Markus himself had been given some leeway in his treatment, if only because it was necessary to get Blodgette to do as she was told. Understandably, she'd utterly refused to get into anything even resembling a van again, so transporting her to the city to be processed had been achieved by loading her and Markus into an open-back logging truck with a very careful driver. They'd made their way to a university that had the proper facilities to treat Blodgette, then Markus had been hauled away for his hearings.

It had all been a blur since then. The legalese being hurled about was several fathoms over his head, and two public defenders had taken a turn representing him before a third lawyer stepped in. That had been a few hours ago. Almost immediately upon this newcomer showing up, Markus had been thrown into his room and left alone with a guard at the door. All information and trial ceased. He wasn't sure if that was a good thing or a bad thing, but at this point he suspected the supply of good things had entirely dried up.

He was still dwelling on just exactly how he'd gotten here and what had happened to his life when the door opened and Gale was led in.

"Markus!" she squealed, relief and excitement in her face as she rushed in to hug him.

"Gale!" he said. "My god, it's good to see you. Do you know what's going on? I haven't heard a thing from a lawyer or a judge in hours!"

"Me neither. This guy, J. S. Hollenger, Esq., shows up and says he's defending me, then boom, they just threw me in a cell. It felt as if I was being sent to the kids' table at Thanksgiving."

"J. S. Hollenger. Is that his name? He didn't even introduce himself."

"That's because he gets paid a couple thousand dollars an hour and I'm a frugal man," said Dimitrios as he stepped through the door.

He was dressed in a *very* sharp outfit, the sort of suit you expected from a lounge singer from the fifties.

"Give us a few minutes alone, would you?" he said to the guard at the door.

The guard nodded and shut the door but did not lock it.

"Uncle Dimitrios, what's going on?" Markus said.

"They say the wheels of justice grind slow, but they grind true. It turns out if you pump a couple hundred thousand dollars into your legal defense, they grind however the hell you want. Or did you forget I'm a millionaire now?"

Markus scratched his head. "I kind of thought that money would sort of go poof once things went south. Wasn't there a contract?"

"You're not a businessman, Markus my boy, so you can be excused for not knowing this. First, contracts involving illegal things are a bear to defend in court. Second, if you've had the... *checkered* entrepreneurial past I've had..."

"You mean one with a couple dozen failed businesses?" Markus said.

"More or less. If you've had a history like that, you get *pretty* good at hiding money." He lowered his voice. "And considering the things the guy who paid me tried to do, the fifteen mill is a *bargain*. Now listen up. Hollenger is finishing things up right now. You're going to be getting off with eight months probation in exchange for some testimony against Grumman."

"Oh, I've got some choice words for *her* all right," Gale said.

"Fine, that's great, but what about Blodgette?" Markus asked.

"Yeah, what about Blodgette?" Gale said.

"I'm getting to that. The legal status of the Struct... the struc..."

"Structophis gastrignae," Gale said.

"Right. The legal status is sort of a gray area with regard to ownership. But the decision has been made that Blodgette will be moved to an animal-behavior facility and education center on the outskirts of Crested Butte to be cared for until her health and psychological state are sufficient that she can be introduced to other... er..."

"Pizza dragons," Markus said.

"Right," Dimitrios agreed.

He knocked on the door, and the guard opened it. The three of them were led out into the hallway.

"There's no facility like that near Crested Butte," Gale said.

Dimitrios dug a freshly printed brochure from his pocket. "There is now! The Spiros Center for Observation, Parenting, and Education. SCOPE!"

Markus took it and flipped through. It was filled with overblown language about the value of learning from the wonders of nature, as well as architectural illustrations of buildings likely not yet built.

"Observation, *Parenting*, and Education?"

"I'll admit, it's a stretch, but these things do better if the acronym spells something."

"Admission, fifteen dollars?" Markus said.

Spiros tapped the page. "Free to schools and kids under twelve. But think of it. There isn't a single facility in the country that'll let the average person come and watch a pizza dragon being raised. And once she's grown, maybe Blodgette will stick around. People might even be able to interact with her! We'll make a fortune, and all for a good cause!"

"I'm sure the good cause is the first thing on your mind," Gale said.

"I'll have you know the *first* thing on my mind was clearing us of potential jail time. To pull that off, I had to make sure that we were able to rehabilitate Blodgette and ensure proper treatment. But don't be so high and mighty. You can't spell SCOPE without 'education.' Paperwork is pending, but by this time next month we'll be an accredited research facility, and we'll be in the market for a head researcher."

"Done!" Gale said, grabbing his hand for a shake. "That's it, hand shake! No take backs! ... What's it pay?"

"A percentage of net receipts. So if I were you, I'd make it interesting enough to pack in the crowds. Think *Crocodile Hunter*."

They reached an exterior door and stepped outside into a parking lot behind the courthouse. A flatbed truck was waiting for them. Blodgette was sitting atop it. Two white-clad handlers were attempting to minister to one of her sore spots, but she had her arms crossed and her head turned aside as though they weren't there.

At the sight of Markus and Gale, she warbled happily and hopped to her feet, then down to the ground—much to the detriment of the pavement. After a few bounding steps she swept Gale and Markus into a tight hug.

"You can thank Blodgette here for probation instead of jail time. They wanted to lock you up, but she refused treatment and we made it clear that if they really cared about her recovery, they'd have to let you two be in charge of it." He turned to the handlers and raised his voice. "See! I told you!"

"What happened to that lady who tried to kill us?" Gale asked.

"She's taking the full brunt of the law. Seems like none of it's flowing uphill to her boss, but that's just the way it goes."

Blodgette released them from the hug and took them each by the hand to lead them up to the back of the flatbed. All sorts of random shapes had been scrawled on the deck of the truck in sidewalk chalk. The dragon proudly pointed to some of them. Her novice artistry meant that it wasn't clear to anyone but her what she'd drawn, but she was clearly very pleased with how it had turned out.

"There're all sorts of handgrips up there, so hold tight! It'll be a few hours before we're to the facility, and I don't want my new research team falling off. The place is basically an empty lot right now with some tents, but you just wait. Before long it'll be the biggest thing to hit the town since my bistro!"

Gale quickly struck up a conversation with the handlers about how Blodgette was doing. Markus sat beside Blodgette and held her hand as she scrawled a fresh picture. Looping, jagged lines traced out the basic shape of a flower.

Markus quietly mused as he watched her. For a long time now he'd been hoping to make something of himself. Night classes, long hours, studying. He was trying to turn himself into the sort of person who could make a difference. Someone who would mean something. It hadn't struck him until this very moment that there was a whole lot more to meaning something than being skilled and doing an important job. No one really meant anything unless they meant it *to* someone. Now there was Blodgette. He meant the world to her, and now it was clear that she meant the world to him.

There was no doubt that his life was a shambles now, but he was okay with that. Sometimes when it feels as though your life has been derailed, it's just because you were stuck on the same track and needed to change course. He never would have imagined that riding on the back of a flatbed with an exotic animal would be the right choice for him, but as Blodgette murmured happily and traced out another flower, he couldn't imagine being anywhere else.

Structophis gastrignae
illustrated by anti-dark-heart

Eggs of the Abbey

A boxy European utility vehicle rumbled along the narrow roads of the Italian coast in the dead of night. The truck looked a bit odd, a wide, flat pickup truck bed attached to an open-backed and canvas-roofed crew cab. Dino, the man at the wheel, was driving with far more care than the many scrapes and dents along the fenders would suggest. In the passenger seat to his left, a portlier gentleman named Antonio gazed out the window. From his expression, he wasn't pleased with what he was seeing.

"Dino, I gotta tell you, when you told me you knew where we could score something big, I expected a city, not the countryside. Is this going to be a heist or a picnic?" Antonio jabbed.

"Yeah, yeah," added the man in the back seat, a squirrelly fellow by the name of Celso, "and I'm looking in this bag of stuff you got here, and it ain't exactly painting pictures of big money."

"I told you not to look in the bag until we got there," Dino growled.

"Hey, Dino, you're lucky I was willing to get in the *truck* without knowing all the details. What's he got in there, Celso?" Antonio said.

Celso rummaged through the bag, amid much clanking and clanging.

"We got a couple balaclavas, so that's promising. But then there's a big pair of tongs and some oven mitts and a puffy apron…"

"*Oh.*" Antonio gave Dino a slap to the back of the head. "Are we robbing a place, or are we baking some cakes?"

"Yeah, yeah. Enough with the spy stuff. What's the plan?" Celso said.

Dino took a hand from the steering wheel to rub his head. "All right. Fine. We're far enough out now, I guess I can tell you. I didn't want to tell you *so* far, because the lady was real clear. Any word of this gets out at all, we ain't getting paid. This only happens if no one finds out until after she gets the goods."

"Who's this lady?" Antonio said.

"I don't know. A German lady. Real businesslike. Almost military I guess."

"Sounds like a cop, Dino. You taking jobs from cops? Trying to get us caught?" Celso said.

"It wasn't a cop," Dino said. "You don't think I can spot a cop when I see one? Like I said. Businesslike. Corporate. Anyway. She said she was *very interested* in some precious stones or something. Antique kind of things. Said there was some sort of an exhibition at that abbey down past Sienna."

"Whoa, hey. We ain't robbing a church, are we?" Antonio said.

"Yeah, yeah," Celso said. "I ain't robbed a church since I was a kid."

"I got a hard enough time fencing jewelry and DVDs and such. Where am I going to unload a religious relic?"

"You listening at *all?* We don't have to worry about how to unload the stuff. I already have a buyer. And it isn't religious relics. It's not church stuff we're stealing. It's just stuff *in* a church."

"Seems like you're splitting hairs. I'm liking this job less and less."

"Yeah, well. It pays 10,000 euros per stone, and there's seven of them."

"I'll believe it when I see it," Antonio said.

"Celso, you see an envelope in the bottom of that bag?"

"Yeah, yeah, I see it."

"Open it up."

He tore open a thick manila envelope.

"Tony, there's like five thousand euros in here."

"Uh-huh. The lady gave me half the money for the first stone up front."

Antonio's eyes opened wide. "Now I like the job."

"I thought you might."

"So, what kind of stones are these? And why are they at a church?"

"I don't know *why* they're there, but they're sort of smooth, round hunks of charcoal. Apparently, they're going to be in the east courtyard."

"Just out in the open?"

"Probably not. She said we should 'anticipate difficulties.' And she also suggested they might be in a furnace or something. Hence the baking equipment."

"A furnace?"

"I thought maybe it was some corporate slang for a high-tech safe, but she meant a literal furnace."

"Weird…"

He shrugged. "Rich corporate types are into weird stuff. Remember that guy who paid us to steal that stuffed beaver from his friend's office? But we've boosted museums, we've cracked safe deposit boxes. What's a church going to throw at us that we can't handle?"

Antonio reached back to grab a mask. "For seventy thousand euros, it'd have to throw an awful lot at us to chase me away."

***

Their truck coasted to a stop down the road from the abbey at 2:15 am. The trio of thieves filed out, each strapped with an assortment of tools of the trade. Bolt cutters, lock-picks, ropes, and empty sacks joined the oven mitts and tongs that made this mission unique.

If they felt a twinge of guilt to be descending upon this hallowed ground, it didn't show on their masked faces. They moved silently through the treed landscape surrounding the quaint and historic grounds. The place was built a bit like a fort, with stout, red brick walls reaching up around them, enclosing a series of internal courtyards. What separated it from a genuine military structure was the relative abundance of fine marble statues, the far more impressive landscaping, and the utter lack of guards or other armed personnel.

Dino stopped at the corner of one of the buildings and slipped a paper map from an inside pocket.

"Should be just on the other side of that wall," he said.

"No cameras. No watchmen. Hard to believe they'd be keeping something in here that'd be worth almost a hundred thousand," Antonio said.

"Yeah, yeah," Celso chimed in. "We ain't even hit a locked door yet."

"You two want to stand around looking gift horses in their mouths until we get caught, or do you want to finish this caper?" Dino hissed. "Come on!"

They moved with the coordination of commandos on a night raid, hustling across the last open walkway and edging up to an arched gate leading to the courtyard. A gentle push at the handles revealed that it was latched from the other side.

"There," Dino said, sliding a knife from his belt. "You happy now. We hit a lock. You two keep watch. I'm going to work on this."

Antonio and Celso moved off to opposite corners and set their eyes on the most likely paths that the authorities might use if they were running patrols. Dino peered through the narrow crack in the louvered gate to see what was waiting for him on the other side. In the light of the moon, he couldn't make out much. It seemed to be little more than another brick-paved quad. It housed a rather out-of-place statue, though. The others they passed were the standard fare for a religious site, monks with solemn faces and strangely oversize hands and the like. This statue was … just *odd*. It had a bulbous pear shape. The color seemed different from the brick. Elements had a terra-cotta look, warmer ochre in contrast to the pale clay elsewhere. He couldn't quite tell what it was supposed to be, as its back was to him. There were thick arms and legs, but also an oddly long neck and a beefy tail curling off to the side.

Rather than waste another few minutes pondering the nuances of monastic artwork, Dino scoped out the rest of the courtyard. Some low tables and platforms were arrayed around the statue, piled with bits of impressively painted ceramic. Tucked in the corner in a burlap-lined tray sat a handful of conspicuous black stones.

He slipped the knife between two slats and jabbed it into the cross-brace holding the gate shut. All it took was a simple, careful slide to ease it aside. When the gate was no longer secured, he scrutinized its edges, seeking wires, magnets, *anything* that might suggest there were alarms or security measures in place. Nothing.

The others gathered behind him again.

"I ain't seen a coast so clear in the last ten jobs we did," Celso whispered. "We may as well be in a city park."

"Seems like they're planning some sort of festival here. There's going to be an art show or something," Antonio said. "I saw some signs up."

"Good. At least that explains why there might be something worth stealing in here," Dino said. "Let's move quick, in and out. Check the near corners for motion detectors and cameras, then to the far left corner to collect the goods."

"Got it," Antonio said.

"Yeah, yeah," Celso agreed.

Dino lifted and pushed the gate to avoid even the potential of a creak. When it was wide enough for them to squeeze through, they one by one slipped into the courtyard. Eyes darted around to all the places smart security designers would hide a sensor, then to all the places stupid security designers would put one. There was nothing. The place had more bird's nests than anti-theft measures.

The moon was overhead, the only source of light. It cast long, sharp shadows of the roofline. The three thieves edged along the wall in the strip of darkness, working toward the tray of precious stones. Antonio reached it first. With gloved hands, he gently lifted one of the matte black stones.

"It looks like an ostrich egg," he mouthed silently.

"Fits the description. Just pack them up and let's get out of here," Dino said.

With skills that would have put a grocery bagger to shame, the trio plucked the grapefruit-size stones, wrapped them in thermal blankets, and slid them into secure sacks. They had underestimated the size of the stones, so the sacks they'd brought weren't quite large enough to securely carry all seven of them. They wordlessly agreed that Dino would hand-carry the final one.

He held the final valuable stone in his hand and puzzled over its nature. It was warm to the touch. Warmer than the night air. And though it was rough and dark as charcoal, it wasn't nearly as sooty. He barely got any of the fine black powder on his fingers as he grasped the lumpy surface. The others would need a few moments more to finish securing their own eggs, so he sidled along the wall to get a better view of the pottery and statue that he'd caught only a glimpse of from the doorway.

Seeing it up close didn't help clarify what it was supposed to be. If the artist had intended it to be a dragon, he'd not tried nearly hard enough. Yes, it had a long neck and a long tail, but the statue seemed far too... *architectural* to be a proper creature. Terra-cotta panels formed a mask on its face and traced out simple armored sections along its shoulders and belly, not unlike the scales of a mythical beast. But there were also hinged metal doors. Four of them, positioned around the perimeter of its potbelly, were little square hatches. The remaining one was a large oval door.

The most distinctive part of the statue was that it seemed to be functional. Small vent slits along the neck and interspersed between the doors had a faint glow, the dull red of the smoldering coals at the end of a campfire. A similar glow emanated from the crack between the central doors in the belly. And the *heat*. Even standing a few paces away he could feel the scalding intensity.

His partners were just finishing up now. Celso had cinched his sacks tight and wandered over to inspect the pottery on the tables. One of the most deeply ingrained instincts in any career thief is the analysis of any and all items for potential value.

"Look at this thing," Celso said, crouching low to rotate one of the larger pots. "It looks like someone used their feet to make this."

Dino didn't take his eyes off the statue to investigate, and it was a good thing he didn't. Celso's criticism was quiet, but not *quite* silent. And his lapse in stealth had been enough to establish something very important about the statue.

It wasn't a statue.

The head twitched. With razor-sharp reflexes, all three men pressed themselves to the walls, dark clothes fading perfectly into the sharp shadow. Slowly, slits in the mask of the creature widened and took on the same smoldering glow as the vents. Then the beak-like maw opened and a long, low yawn shook the courtyard. The thieves dare not move now that the creature's eyes were open. Any motion at *all* would reveal them.

It raised a thick arm and rubbed at its eyes, producing a stone-on-stone grind, then looked down at its belly. With pudgy fingers, it pinched the latch and raised it, pivoting open the doors to release a potent blast of heat from within. It reached inside and carefully removed a pot quite like the others set around it on the tables. With care and delicacy one would think was impossible for something so large, it placed the still faintly glowing pot on a small stone platform to cool.

The creature closed its belly door. After a moment to admire the pot, it glanced aside. It leaned lower, shuffling its legs out from under it and placing its palms on the ground to inspect the very table Celso had been investigating. It reached out and pinched the top of the pot he'd critiqued, twisting it to return it to its original orientation, then gazed into the darkness.

Lesser thieves would have lost their nerve. The thing, which at this point could only be called a dragon, was looking right at them. But it hadn't reacted yet, which meant its vision couldn't penetrate the darkness. It couldn't see them, and if they held their ground they *might* just escape notice.

The thing stretched its neck forward and took a deep breath. The sound was like the bellows on a great forge. And *like* a forge, as the hot breath hissed back out through its nostrils, the flames within were stoked. The heat grew more intense. The glow flared ... and revealed Dino.

For a terrifying moment, all was still. Burning eyes fixed on the terrified burglar. Then those eyes shifted downward and settled on the stone he held. Pieces fell into place in his mind, just as they did in the mind of the creature. These weren't hunks of charcoal. They weren't odd carvings or precious stones. They didn't just *look* like eggs. They *were* eggs. And this was their mother.

It was astonishing how effectively two simple slits in a terra-cotta mask could express the raw, unparalleled fury of a protective mother seeing its young threatened. Dino opened his mouth to warn the others to run, but the slap of the gate and the patter of departing footsteps revealed they'd been a bit quicker on the draw than he had been.

Dino broke into a sprint, springing over a sweeping tail that shattered through the pottery before her like a wrecking ball. The dragon screeched, the sound like a cross between a pterodactyl and a steam whistle. He dared not look back, pouring every ounce of his mind and body into escaping this courtyard with his ill-gotten gains.

The ground rattled beneath his feet as adrenaline coursed through his veins, allowing him to close the gap between himself and his fleeing friends. They burst between the trees, Dino clutching the loose egg like a rugby ball as he fumbled for the keys in his pocket. The dragon burst *through* the trees, the ele-phant-size behemoth flattening topiaries and roaring in anger.

In the distance, the raised voices of the people of the abbey bellowed to one another in anger and confusion.

"It's after *me!*" Dino called, tossing the keys to Antonio. "I'll try to lead it away. You start the truck and double back!"

Antonio caught the keys. He and Celso vanished among the thicker foliage. Dino leapt a shallow gully and ran for his life. He emerged on a narrow footpath leading back to the main road. A blast of splintered wood assured him that the dragon was barely steps behind him. He wouldn't be able to stay ahead, so he zagged toward the abbey again, running parallel to the main road.

The buildings of the abbey approached. And beyond them, the parking lot. He could hear the engine of his beat-up old utility vehicle flaring to life in the distance. He could *also* hear the rattle of the metal doors and the enraged hiss of breath of the monster hot on his tail.

Just as the hissing breath began to sizzle the back of his mask, he slid into a tight alley between two of the buildings of the abbey. The dragon ground to a stop. It screeched again and reached into the alley with its doughy paw.

He edged along as the vocalizations of the creature oscillated between spine-tingling rage and heart-wrenching anxiety. In the parking lot ahead, his truck skidded into view and pulled a 180-degree turn that nearly caused it to overturn. The dragon's gaze shifted to the truck.

Dino dashed out of the far end of the alleyway. Celso threw the tailgate open and leaned out, his hand extended. The dragon rounded the edge of the building and rapidly closed the gap. Wheels screeched and peeled out. Dino leapt and barely caught the grip of his partner in crime. He dragged his feet on the asphalt. The egg under his arm nearly came free. Celso hauled him inside a split-second before the sweeping head of the enraged dragon struck the open tailgate, tearing it free from the truck.

For a few heart-stopping moments it seemed like the dragon would overtake them. Her heaving breath caused patches of the paint of the truck to blister and peel. But slowly the vehicle's acceleration and the beast's fatigue finally gave them the edge.

It roared one last time before they screeched around a turn and onto the main road.

***

"What *was* that thing? What on earth *was* that thing?" stammered Antonio as he struggled to stay on the road while pushing the truck to its limits.

"I don't know! But it's definitely the sort of thing you'd have to pay tens of thousands of euros for someone to steal something from it!" Dino said.

"Yeah, yeah. You better get that money, Dino. No one said we'd be fighting dinosaurs," Celso chimed in.

Dino and Celso each climbed over the back seat to a place where they were marginally less likely to be thrown from the rear of the truck. They stowed the stray egg.

"We've got company," Antonio said.

Flashing lights were visible in the distance as police closed in.

"Where are we dropping these things off? They are red-hot now. Let's just get our money and get out!" he said.

"Yeah, yeah. I don't want to be sitting on a big pile of dinosaur eggs," said Celso.

"They're not dinosaur eggs!" Dino barked, fumbling for his phone.

"Well what *are* they?" Celso asked.

Dino flipped open his phone and scrolled through his contacts. "I… I don't know… *Dragon* eggs, I guess."

"Because that's *so* much more sane and reasonable, Dino," Antonio growled. "Just make the call!"

He finally found the contact he had been given and hit send. The phone rang a few times. A calm, measured voice answered.

"Hello, Dino."

"Listen! We've got the eggs."

"Who said anything about eggs?"

"Those stones you wanted were eggs! And I *know* they were, because the mother went on a *rampage* when we took them. You could have *told* me we were stealing dragon eggs. We would have prepared more!"

"If you will recall, information security was key for this operation. I provided you with the information necessary to successfully locate and identify the targets. And to be perfectly frank, it speaks poorly of your professionalism if you must be coaxed into approaching a job with a proper level of preparation."

"Cops are getting closer, Dino. I need a direction so I can start losing them," Antonio said.

"Fine, whatever. We got them all. All seven. So where do we drop them off to get our payment?"

"I must reiterate, Dino. Information security was key. I could not have any credible thread connecting the acquisition of these items with their delivery."

"You *won't*. We'll lose the police and you'll be clean."

"I have people monitoring local police communications. Apparently, you left your tailgate behind."

"Yeah, so?"

"Your license plate was still attached. Imagine my surprise when I heard them reciting your registration information. Surely even a mid-level criminal would have used an unregistered vehicle."

"Listen, lady! We stole these eggs for *you*. And the only way you're getting them is if you—"

"The terms of the agreement were clear, Dino. The police know who you are and what you have. That is unacceptable to us. Consider the contract terminated. You are free to keep the initial payment. Good-bye."

Before he could hurl the salvo of profanities she'd inspired, she hung up. He furiously redialed, but found that in the moments since she'd hung up, the phone number had become disconnected.

"That didn't sound good," Antonio said.

"Head south. We're going to Naples."

"Naples! That's at least four hours away!" Antonio said.

"You'll probably *need* that long to lose the cops anyway."

"Why are we going to Naples? What's with the lady?"

"She's stiffing us because the cops got wise to us. So we're going to sell this to Vin's uncle. Carlo."

"Carlo! That guy bargains like the devil. We aren't getting seventy thousand euros out of *him*."

"No, but we'll get *something*."

"We'll be lucky if we can get gas money out of him."

"Yes, Tony, we *will* be lucky if we can get gas money out of him. Because people willing to fence *exotic animal eggs* are a little hard to come by. But if anyone I know can swing it, it's Carlo."

"I don't know..."

"Do you have a better idea?"

The getaway driver glanced in the rear-view mirror at the police. With a grumble of frustration, he swerved aside and spun the truck toward the south.

***

Several years later...

An elderly but spry man walked along the streets of Naples. He couldn't have screamed 'tourist' more effectively unless he had chosen to do so vocally. His outfit was fresh from a local clothing store, so fresh that the belt still bore its price tag. He had a large digital camera hanging around his neck and was too busy looking at the scenery to watch where he was going.

After bumping into his third local, he paused in front of an innocuous store with crowded windows. On the door was a hand-lettered sign declaring it *Antiquariato di Carlo*. He pulled out a comically fat wallet and slipped up a business card with a smudged note with the same address. He stepped inside.

The place was heaped with antiques, their quality ranging from utterly ancient and eroded cameras that would never function again to gold-leafed picture frames that didn't appear to have aged a day in the hundreds of years since they were crafted. Of all the many and varied objects in the shop, the one which looked the most antiquated was the owner.

He was a tiny, spindly man. Though his customer was easily in his eighties, the shop owner had to have been fifteen years his senior. He was bent almost double, his face drawn and hawkish. Beady eyes stared through, small, round lenses nearly as thick as they were wide. He was perched atop a tall stool behind a counter, a jeweler's loupe held to his eye as he appraised a pocket watch. When he looked up, he cast the same appraising eye upon the tourist. From the sour turn his expression took, he did not anticipate getting very much value from this transaction.

"Hola, Parli Englisch?" said the customer.

The shopkeeper tipped his head to the side.

"I speak English," he replied, his accent thick and his voice wispy. "I hope you do as well, sir, because you don't seem to have a firm grasp on your Spanish, Italian, or German."

"Sure, sure. Greek is the native tongue, but English is the language of business, so that's what I speak."

There was little evidence to suggest Greek was his native tongue. His accent was unmistakably—if somewhat generically—American. He also spoke with the boisterous and genial mannerisms one tended to associate with Americans, for better or worse. The man extended his hand for a shake.

"Dimitrios Spiros. Entrepreneur," he said. "You must be Carlos."

"Carlo. How may I help you, Mr. Spiros?" the shopkeeper said.

"I'm not so sure. Seems like you've got a lot of old stuff in here, Carlos."

"Yes, sir. It is an *antique* shop."

"Even so," Dimitrios said, picking up an old clock to investigate. "But even by those standards, this stuff seems a little *too* old. Back home, antique shops go back to maybe the 1940s."

"We … have more history here in Europe."

"How much more history is really worth *having?* You ask me, everything has been working up to, and down from, the 1960s."

"A relief that no one has asked you, then. What exactly are you looking for?"

"I own a bistro back in the states. Neighborhood place. I'm looking for something to really make us pop. You know. Stand out."

"May I suggest some fine furniture ..." Carlo said, stiffly stepping down from his stool and approaching an elegant table with two finely made chairs. "Something of this design? I do not keep enough inventory to supply an entire eatery, but with enough time I can find you a set of the proper size."

Dimitrios rocked the chair back and forth. "Not for me. The Naugahyde is holding up fine. Nothing a few patches can't fix."

Carlo's opinion of his customer, impressively, managed to fall a few more notches.

"I think, perhaps, you should look elsewhere."

"I'm sure you have got *something* good."

"Good is a matter of taste, Mr. Spiros. I am not sure you would know it if you saw it."

The jab bounced off him, completely unnoticed. From the expression on his face, in his mind he'd already wandered three or four topics away from the conversation.

"Oh!" he said, snapping his fingers. "I was supposed to tell you. Giovanni sent me."

Carlo's expression remained stony. "I do not know anyone named Giovanni."

"If you're Carlos, you know Giovanni. He's on the other side of town. Said you carry some, ahem, *special* items."

The shopkeeper now reappraised the visitor.

"What sort of special items did you have in mind?"

Dimitrios glanced about a bit theatrically to ensure there was no one else in a store that barely had enough free space for the two of them.

"Let's lay it all out there. You and I both know the best stuff is the stuff you aren't *supposed* to sell. And I only buy the best stuff."

Carlos briefly considered the possibility that this was a sting. But no police officer in the history of law enforcement could possibly be as clumsy and incompetent at entrapment as this person would have to be if he was anything less than sincere.

But there were other reasons besides fear of legal issues to avoid
doing business with someone.

"I do not have anything that might make a bistro 'pop.' You
would be better off looking elsewhere."

Dimitrios removed a knot of currency from his pocket and
thumped it down on the antique table.

"You let me decide that. I know quality when I see it."

Carlo looked to the wad of money. It was at least four thousand Euros, and the conservative nature with which he'd revealed
it suggested there was a good deal more where it came from. His
body language alone suggested Carlo had shifted from working
out how best to remove this oaf from his store to how to most
effectively part the fool from his money in the process.

"What sort of bistro is this, sir?"

"We have a full menu of top quality, multi-ethnic cuisine. But
what I'm really working on is building up my pizza delivery side
business. And where better than Italy to find something for that,
right? Nothing says pizza like Italy, Carlos."

Carlo shut his eyes. "Before we do business, a few questions.
First, you seem to be interested in something which challenges
the limits of legality."

"I want something that goes right past legal. Like I said.
That's where the good stuff is."

"How do you hope to help your business with something that,
if discovered, would put you on the wrong side of the law?"

"You let *me* worry about that. I'm an entrepreneur, like I said.
Things are only illegal until they aren't. Shouldn't let that get in
the way of good business."

After a few more moments of consideration, Carlo grinned.

"I believe I have something for you."

He disappeared through a curtain in the back. A few moments later, he returned a large box with assorted dials and me-
ters on it. It looked a bit like a particularly complex humidor.
The shopkeeper's thin fingers danced across its latches and locks,
then lifted the lid to reveal seven recesses, two of which were still
occupied with rough, matte black eggs.

"Are you aware of the *Structophis gastrignae?*" he asked.

"Sounds contagious," Dimitrios quipped.

"Common name is Pizza Dragon. A vanishingly rare species. Incubated inside a pizza oven, upon emergence, they grow to incorporate the oven. A union of creature and mechanism. The subject of endless study and scientific curiosity."

Carlo slid a booklet from beneath the case and handed it to Dimitrios. As the customer leafed through pages of photographs, anatomical illustrations, and articles, he continued the sales pitch.

"In all of modern history, no individual has ever *owned* one of these creatures. At least, not publicly. That is because, in all modern history, there has never been a single egg that has not been accounted for by scientists and conservationists... except for this set."

"Where are the rest?"

"If someone were to come in here and ask me where *you* were, after purchasing this, would you want me to identify you?"

"I suppose not."

He leafed through the pages of the booklet and held up an image of a full-grown creature, a being of doughy flesh and clay brick.

"Look at that!" Dimitrios said. "Now that says 'artisanal' to me. One of those standing outside my place... That'd pack them in... Give it a snappy name, make some merchandise. T-shirts. Stuffed animals. It'd be the next Noid."

"In the hands of a visionary, I am sure the sky is the limit."

"It says here it'll take a few years before it's walking around..."

"Yes, sir. They have rather rigid and complex requirements to be raised into healthy specimens."

"Bah. All good investments take time to ripen. I'll take one. What's the price?"

Carlo glanced to the table, then looked Dimitrios over.

"For something this rare? I could not imagine letting it go for less than fifteen thous—"

"Sold," Dimitrios said, pulling a second wad of cash from his pocket and peeling off the appropriate amount.

Carlo winced at the thought of how much higher he could have set the price. Dimitrios handed the booklet back.

"No, sir. You will need that. Remember, the care and feeding are very particular."

"Right. Right. The user's manual. Now, now... which one to choose..."

He picked one up and hefted it, then did the same to the other. To all outward appearances, he may as well have been picking out a cantaloupe.

"This one. Heavy for its size. Wrap it up to go. It'll be my carry-on when I go home." He smiled as he handed it over. "And take good care of it. That right there is how Dimitrios Spiros makes his fortune ..."

A Big Day for Blodgette

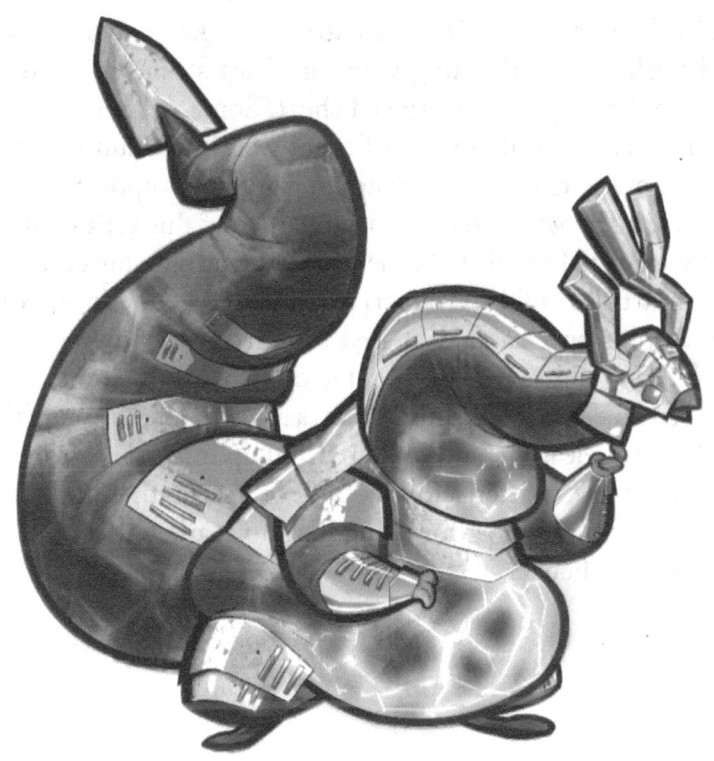

Structophis gastrignae
illustrated by ProjectENDO

Introduction

What follows is part of the "Shorts of Dubious Canonicity" project I started in 2018. In an attempt to keep my mind sharp and fresh, I started taking votes on short stories to write each weekend. Some of them stayed short. Some of them grew into full novellas. But almost all of them were the result of my fans and followers casting their votes to give them support.

Pizza Dragon is the unofficial name for this series. I'd never really expected much to come of it. In truth, it started as a gift for an artist I follow, ProjectENDO. He is the creator of the Structophis species, and at first I didn't expect to write a full book. It would just be a chapter or two to give him. Then it grew to an entire book, but I still wasn't sure I'd release it. Then I decided to release it, and to help drum up interest, I wrote a prequel. Now I've written a follow-up! For a series that has basically become a running gag for being hard to market, it certainly has found its audience.

A Big Day for Blodgette

A phone buzzed from its perch on a bedside table. After two more buzzes, a hand thrust out from beneath a mound of blankets and felt around for the bothersome device. Markus Spiros lifted his head and blinked his eyes blearily at the device. It took him another buzz before he realized that this was a phone call, not an alarm.

He answered. "Eee-yaugh…"

It was as near to a word as he could manage on such short notice.

"Hey, I'm at the gate and I forgot my pass. Buzz me in," said a frustratingly chipper voice on the other side of the line.

"Gale?" he muttered, sleep gradually clearing from his brain.

"Yeah! Hurry up. I'm carrying a bunch of stuff."

She didn't wait for confirmation, she just hung up. Markus released a few more sounds that probably would have been rude if he'd been able to wrangle the diction to form them properly. He climbed out of bed and hastily got dressed.

This wasn't his old apartment. It looked more like a dorm room or a particularly luxurious jail cell. He had a bed and a nightstand, a desk with a computer, and a dresser with a TV perched atop it. There wasn't really room for anything else. He grabbed a comb from the nightstand and slipped his sandals on before heading out the door. Before it shut, he ducked back in and grabbed a lanyard with a photo ID hanging from it.

A florescent-lit hallway awaited him on the other side of this door. It still had the weird odors of recently completed construction. He pushed opened a door across the hall to reveal another suitably dorm-like bathroom and shower facility. With Gale waiting at the gate there was no time for a proper morning routine, but he dragged the comb across his head and washed his face so that he would look a little less zombie-like for the trek across the facility.

Markus trudged through the visitor's center. It was brightly colored and scattered with freshly printed posters containing the schedule for future events. Stuffed dragons of various descriptions lined shelves in the gift kiosk to one side. He nodded to an employee in an apron and paper hat that made her look like a chef from a 1960s greasy spoon.

"Morning, Mr. Spiros," the young woman said brightly. "Today's the big day, huh?"

"Yeah," he said, fighting off a yawn. "Today's the big day."

He continued walking as the statement bounced off a brain not yet functional enough to process it. He swiped his badge and wandered through two more hallways before he came to the employee entrance and buzzed it open. It had barely slid open a crack when a boot jabbed into the opening and swung it fully open.

"Up and at 'em, sleepyhead!" crowed the young woman who had been waiting.

His friend and collaborator, Gale Dekker, perpetually had the sort of exuberant, amped-up attitude that could only result from a steady diet of caffeine. She had a shirt with a manatee on it, khaki cargo shorts, and her arms were heavily loaded with goodies.

"Coffee and donuts," she said, holding out the to-go tray she'd gotten from the local breakfast joint.

He took the tray and held the door as she sidled in. The rest of her cargo was a seemingly random assortment. She had a planter with a flowering stalk wrapped about a wire frame. Some smaller plants were in their own plastic pots tucked in around it. The crook of her arm had a plastic bag with various cured meats emerging from it.

"It's the big day!" she said, handing over enough of her goods to make navigating the hallway a less precarious enterprise.

"Big day," he repeated mechanically.

He sniffed the non-iced coffee in the tray and managed to take a sip from it without removing it.

"Big day," he said again, this time actually trying to attach meaning to the words.

"Yeah! Final inspection. Don't tell me you forgot."

He blinked as the realization came tumbling out of his brain.

"Oh, right. Yeah. Yeah, big day."

"I'm *amazed* at how quick your uncle got this place together. Built in three months, almost ready to *run* in six."

"He's got experience getting things put together in a hurry. Since most of his enterprises don't last more than a year, the less of that year you spend under construction, the better."

"I think this one's going to last. The Spiros Center for Observation, Parenting, and Education; Head Researcher: Gale Dekker."

"Uh-huh. You know, the rules of nepotism normally require that the boss's nephew get the head position."

"You *do* have the head position. Head caretaker. That's the more important job anyway. This place is *all* about Blodgette. How's she doing this morning?"

"Sleeping. Like I was supposed to be for another 45 minutes."

"The earlier the start, the better! Let's go see her."

They took a different route through the building, eventually coming to a room with a large glass window facing what appeared to be something between a large animal paddock, a community garden, and an outdoor bistro. It was open air, with chain-link fences separating it from a ten-foot grass walkway and then a tall cement wall. The fences were thick with hanging planters and climbing vines. Each held a different flowering plant: marigolds, lavender, chamomile. Designated sections of the ground had raised beds with tomato plants, rose bushes, and sunflowers.

An artificial pond took up about half of the rear of the enclosure, and led under the edge of a tall awning that shaded the entryway to a high-roofed shelter with large sliding doors. Markus waved his badge over a reader and bumped open an employee-only door, then paced his way to a gate in the chain-link fence.

"Blodgette!" he called. "Time to get started!"

The ground trembled and, somewhere deep inside the shelter, a resounding metallic rattle and clunk rang out. Then came an excited, burbling trill. The heavy door to the shelter rumbled open. From the darkness within, two smoldering eyes peered out.

What came waddling out probably would have been terrifying if not for how genuinely delighted it appeared to be. Blodgette had grown in the last six months. Not much, at least by dragon standards, probably a few hundred pounds and six inches or so. Her former home and current armor—the remains of a pair of steel pizza ovens—was almost unrecognizable now. Her unique physiology had taken it several steps further from its appliance origins and a good deal closer to the samurai-esque armor plating it had only weakly resembled in the earliest days. A gleaming stainless steel mask somehow failed to conceal the broad grin on her muzzle. She thumped toward Markus with her arms wide.

He hastily put down the things he'd been holding. A few months of seeing Blodgette every morning had taught him there was no stopping the morning hug. She scooped him up in her pudgy arms and rocked back and forth. Gale dropped her things as well, eager to grab the camera that was perpetually around her neck so that she could snap some pictures.

"It's only been six hours, Blodgette. This isn't a grand reunion," he said.

Blodgette dropped Markus and waddled back, hands held out in front of her. When Markus took a step toward her, she trilled once and motioned with her hands again.

"Fine, fine. I'll wait here," he said.

The dragon rubbed her stubby hands together, then took a breath. She tapped the fingers of one hand against her chin, waved it once toward her, then turned the palm forward and jabbed her thumb twice against her chin. Markus smirked.

"That means 'Good morning, Mom.' Are you *sure* you wanted to say that?"

Blodgette nodded eagerly. Markus sighed. Since their earliest experiments in communication, Blodgette had gotten the thought lodged in her head that the right word for Markus was "mom." They'd taken great pains to try to make the meaning of the word clear to her, and to suggest alternatives, but Blodgette was firm in her insistence that despite all of that, Markus was Mom.

The dragon turned to Gale. She had switched from photos to shooting video. Blodgette repeated the same wave, but this time concluded it by swirling both hands about in the air. Gale nearly dropped the camera.

"Oh my gosh, oh my gosh, oh my gosh!" Gale squealed. "She said good morning to me! And I think I know that sign."

She grabbed her phone and navigated to an American Sign Language dictionary.

"Wind! She said, 'Good morning, Wind'! Did you teach her that?" Gale asked.

"It was her idea. We were working on spelling your name out and she was frustrated. One thing led to another and we ended up looking up the word that came closest."

"A *Structophis gastrignae* gave me a nickname!" she said, hopping up and down.

Blodgette raised her hand expectantly.

"Yes, you get a high five for that, bring it down here!" Gale said, raising her own hand.

They clapped hands and Blodgette chirped proudly, then looked at the assortment of new things the two caretakers had brought.

"Oh, yes. These are for you," Gale said.

Blodgette delicately removed all of the smaller planters and lined them up, then picked up the largest one to sniff at the odd-shaped yellow bloom.

She set the planter down and signed.

Flower.

"That's right," Markus said. "Flower."

"It's a squash flower," Gale added. "Squash. Like this."

Gale worked her way laboriously through the letters of the word. American Sign Language was just as new to her as to Markus and Blodgette, but she'd made it a point to become fluent in at least the letters. The dragon blinked at her as she went through the motions, then repeated the only important part back at her.

Flower.

Every *Structophis gastrignae*, or Pizza Dragon, as most people called them, eventually picked something to horde. They tended heavily toward edible or culinary items. As the decor of her pen suggested, Blodgette had quickly decided that flowers were worth collecting. Through some not-yet-fully understood instinct or mechanism, she'd illustrated a strong preference toward edible flowers. Not edible to *her* necessarily, but a part of human cuisine in some way. She loved all flowers, but given the choice between something that would look good in a bouquet and something that would look good in a salad, she always chose the entrée.

She worked her way through the others. Gale gave the full name of each plant. Blodgette dubbed it *flower* and found a place for it in the raised beds and hanging pots. Then she came to the tray of donuts and correctly surmised they were for Markus. She handed the tray to him and patiently waited.

"Yes, Blodgette. Thank you," he said.

He knew what she wanted, but sometimes it was fun to make her work for it. She poked the tray, then pinched all of her fingers together and tapped her mouth with them.

Eat.

She planted her fists on her chubby hips and waited again. When Markus had taken a bite of a donut, she nodded once, then waddled toward the pond to wade in. When she was entirely submerged, water hissed against the antler-like metal horns jutting off the top of her mask. She remained submerged until the hissing stopped, then popped to the surface again and shook the water from her head.

Gale took some notes.

"Do you always eat breakfast in here?" she asked.

"No. But if I ever bring food in here that she knows isn't for her, everything stops until she sees that I've eaten some. It's not until recently that she stopped trying to get me to eat the oak logs and chunks of ore we keep in here for her."

"Such powerful nurturing behavior at such a young age..." She scribbled some more notes.

She sniffed, then glanced at him. "You haven't showered at all."

"No, I haven't. Because someone woke me up before my alarm to answer the door. You know there are people in the lobby, right? They could have let you in."

"But they don't have access to Blodgette. Look, it doesn't matter, go get yourself ready. The official from the preservation society is going to be here in two hours and you need to be at your best. I'll keep Blodgette busy and then we'll start getting her ready."

"You hear that, Blodgette?" he called. "Ol' Wind here is going to keep you company. I'll be back in two shakes."

Blodgette bobbed in the water, splashing as she raised a hand to sign.

Goodbye, Mom.

He paced to the gate, then through the facility. For six months, he'd been living with Blodgette. First in a tent on the land that would become this facility, then in the skeleton of the facility as it was built around them. During that time, his Great-Uncle Dimitrios had been busy leaping through legal hoops. Blodgette was an extremely rare creature. Her presence in the country was the result of an illegal action, and her upbringing had been less than ideal. In the beginning, charges of everything from grand theft to child endangerment could have been heaped upon them. Her uncle and his questionably scrupulous lawyer had untied most of those knots. Markus didn't know or care just how that was achieved. Having something more important to focus on has a way of making even potentially life-ruining criminal proceedings seem pointless by comparison. Today was the last hurdle, and as he stood alone in the shower, the full weight of it was coming down upon his shoulders.

A representative from the international governing body for all things *Structophis* was on her way. Markus had spoken to her on the phone at least three times already. Each time it felt like he was having a job interview with someone who'd decided before he walked in the door that he 'wasn't right for this company.' A lot hinged upon how things went today. If he was found to be an unfit caregiver, if Blodgette's health wasn't up to snuff, if her development was too slow, and even if the enclosure wasn't up to their requirements, they could decide that she should be taken away. That had financial consequences for Uncle Spiros—who had sunk much of his recently acquired wealth into the construction of this science center/tourist trap with Blodgette as its only attraction. It had legal consequences for Gale and Markus, each of whom were avoiding fines and jail time in part for their role in taking care of Blodgette.

Oddly, the only things that Markus found himself worrying about were the consequences for Blodgette herself. There was a reason Markus had agreed to *live* at the science center. For the first few months, Blodgette was timid and anxious around anyone else, with the possible exception of Dimitrios. Gale had eventually earned her trust, but even she couldn't calm the beast down if she got worked up. Blodgette had bonded with Markus and that gave him a solid and irreplaceable role in her life for at least the next two years. By then, Blodgette's mind and body would have worked their way toward something approaching adulthood, and she would become more fully self-reliant. But to lose Markus before then would be like tearing a child from its parents.

He finished his shower, brushed his teeth, and put on a fresh uniform. When he returned to the enclosure, he found Gale illustrating why Blodgette's patience for her was so limited.

The two were playing with clay. More accurately, Blodgette was trying to play with clay and Gale was narrating the copious valuable scientific observations of the act while Blodgette glared at her for not participating.

"As you can see, we've got easels set up with pictures of other *Structophis gastrignae*. Today we are trying to get Blodgette to sculpt one."

Play, Blodgette signed, her expression flat and irritated.

"Communal activities are extremely important for *Structophis gastrignae* at this stage of intellectual development. Blodgette's intelligence at this stage is somewhere between that of a five-year-old and an eight-year-old, so she is more than capable of engaging in this activity alone now that she has been shown how. But she is happier and more engaged when others involve themselves as well."

Play, Blodgette signed again, waggling her pinkies a bit more emphatically.

Markus walked over and plopped down beside Blodgette and grabbed a handful of the modeling clay.

"Make sure you take notes on the North American Large Animal Zoologist, one of the most intelligent species in the animal kingdom who for some reason still can't take a hint and just sit down to sculpt a kitty cat," he said.

"Someone's got to do the research, Markus."

"Fine. You do that, I'll be Mom."

He looked up at the easel.

"What do you say we try to make that guy, Blodgette? That's Easy. Sort of the unofficial ambassador of Pizza Dragons. Poster boy for the species."

The creature he'd indicated was indeed quite famous, as Pizza Dragons went. If you knew anything about the species, and not very many people did, you at least knew about Easy. Looking at the creature, you could see why someone might be concerned for Blodgette's health. The two had at least a similar body shape, but for lack of a better term, Blodgette just looked a bit *wrong*. Easy's oven-like components were the proper ones, a little metal in the mask region, but the rest were brick and clay. He had a long, straight neck rather than the stubbier, more kinked neck Blodgette had. His tail was a little thinner and a bit longer than hers and, again, lacked the worrisome kinks. The other big difference was the color of his skin. He had a soft, doughy appearance to his natural hide. Blodgette's skin had improved overall but was still much darker and a bit more craggy. She looked worlds better than she'd looked on her emergence day, but a long way from being the ideal for her species.

Blodgette wadded and squished clay into a chubby snake shape, holding it up to the image frequently to compare. Markus started working on limbs for her creation.

Gale cleared her throat to get his attention, then pointedly glanced at Blodgette. Markus nodded and sighed.

"So, Blodgette. How do you feel lately?" he asked.

With both of her hands busy, she chirped pleasantly in response.

"There's a lady coming today to check you out."

Blodgette gave a less enthusiastic chirp.

"She's going to do a lot of the Gale stuff. Checking your temperature, weighing you. That sort of thing. Lots of pictures."

The dragon huffed.

"I know, I know. No fun. But she's a lady who knows more about pizza dragons than pretty much anyone. She's going to make sure you're okay."

Blodgette nodded.

"You know we all want to make sure you grow up to be the best you can, right?"

She felt around her for a stick and used it to poke some eyes and draw some lines on the surface of the clay.

"She's using tools again!" Gale quietly enthused.

"So if she decides you'd be better off, say, with other Pizza Dragons, you might be taking a trip."

Blodgette snapped her gaze toward him. She set down her clay on the clean tray they'd given her and began to sign.

Bus?

"No. We all know you don't like buses and vans."

She thought for a moment.

Flat bus?

"Probably."

We go?

"Probably you'd go and meet new people and dragons."

We go. This time the "we" part was fairly emphatic. It wasn't a question anymore.

"That's not really up to me. I mean. Let's be clear. It might not happen. I hope it doesn't. But if it *does* happen, do what they say. It's for the best."

Blodgette shook her head. It wasn't an angry motion, just a simple statement that she would not, in fact, be cooperating.

He tried to come up with a more palatable way to introduce the concept to her, but before he could, the intercom system beeped.

"Dr. Morella has arrived."

Gale checked her watch. "She's early."

"I think that's a child services thing. Show up a little early so people have less time to prepare."

"You ready?"

"Ready as I'll ever be."

Gale trotted over to the gate and stepped through to access the PA. There *had* been a PA panel in the enclosure, but Blodgette had found it and serenaded the entire facility with her chirping and trilling until they locked it out.

"Send her in."

"The lady is here now, Blodgette. Be nice, okay."

Play?

"She *might* play."

The woman appeared a moment later. She gave the immediate impression, both in her expression and her wardrobe, of a woman dispatched from the library to reprimand you for your overdue books. Markus looked at her.

"I don't think she'll be playing," he said quietly.

He climbed to his feet and wiped off his hands.

"Dr. Morella?" he said.

"Yes. And you are Mr. Spiros, correct?" she said, with a mild Italian accent.

They shook hands.

"That's right. Markus Spiros. You can call me Markus. And what should I call you?"

"Dr. Morella."

"Right…"

She turned to Gale. "And you are Ms. Dekker?"

"Gale Dekker. Hoping to be Dr. Gale Dekker if I can complete my research."

"I have read your papers. They were quite thorough."

"Thank you!"

"And this is… *Blodgette.*" Her lip curled in the flicker of a sneer as she uttered the name. "I am not overly pleased with the name. It is more appropriate for a pet than a creature of her caliber."

"I hadn't really been thinking about the long term when I came up with it."

"I would be very surprised to discover you did much thinking of the long term at all, Mr. Spiros." She didn't bother looking from Blodette to Markus when she delivered the jab.

The dragon looked uncertainly at Dr. Morella. She climbed to her feet but didn't offer up the hug or anticipate the high five that she did for Markus and Gale. The doctor pulled a tablet from her bag and raised it to snap some pictures of Blodgette.

The dragon huffed and grabbed Markus, gently lifting him and placing him between her and the newcomer before huddling down as though she could hide behind the much smaller human.

"She is inadequately socialized," Dr. Morella said. From her tone, one would think 'inadequate' was the most heinous of indictments.

"She's a little skittish around newcomers. Particularly strangers with cameras," Markus explained.

She marked down Markus's input. The tap of her finger was a bit more forceful than it needed to be. "That is a problem, is it not? As you are hoping to soon have many hundreds of people per day who fit that precise description."

"She's gotten very comfortable *in her enclosure*," Gale clarified. "It's just that you're in here with her."

"*Structophis gastrignae* are extremely social creatures. She should be *very* comfortable with outsiders."

"As you know, she's had sort of a rough few years."

"I am quite aware." Again she avoided looking Markus in the eye when she spoke. She thumped her fingers against the tablet like she was punishing it for being party to this endeavor. "I believe I will begin by assessing the enclosure. Ms. Dekker, if you'll help me?"

Blodgette watched, strafing around Markus to keep her on the far side.

"Come on, Blodgette," Markus said. "Let's go inside and play with your blocks."

"I shall be checking in there next," Dr. Morella said.

"Let's just stand here and wait for the nice lady, Blodgette," he amended.

Gale and the doctor paced around. They stretched a tape measure from every conceivable position to every other position. She measured the PH and temperature of the water, recorded the species of every plant, and even took samples of the grass.

Blodgette tapped his shoulder. He turned to her.

Play?

"Let's wait until the nice lady is done, shall we?"

Blodgette chirped unhappily and turned to the bags Gale had brought. She found the meats. Though the pepperonis and salamis were full size deli-meats, in her hands they looked like the sort of meat snack you'd find beside the cash register in a gas station. She took a bite of one, then after a moment, paced over to the doctor and offered an entire salami to her.

Dr. Morella raised her eyebrows at the offer, but she was, after all, a professional when it came to these creatures. Rather than turn down the offer, she pulled a small knife from her bag, cut off a piece of the meat, and ate it.

"Thank you very much, Blodgette," she said, with all the cordiality of a person being introduced to royalty. "I think we know enough about the enclosure. Let's have a look at you."

Dr. Morella took a few pictures from a few different angles.

"To the scale, please."

"Let's go, Blodgette," Markus said.

They paced over and the dragon obediently stood on the scale. More measurements were taken. Dr. Morella tried to swab her skin at one point, but that crossed a line of personal space that convinced Blodgette to grab Markus again, clutching him like a teddy bear and waddling back a few steps every time Dr. Morella tried to close the gap and try again.

"If you would, Mr. Spiros."

"Come on, Blodgette. The sooner it's over, the sooner we can do story time."

Blodgette huffed a breath with the edge of a grumble beneath it. She relented and let Markus go. He performed that test, as well as the internal temperature check and a few simple imitation exercises to check flexibility.

"The last thing I'd like to assess is mental acuity," Dr. Morella said. "She seems to have a firm understanding of the English language."

"She understands everything we say if we speak simply," Markus said.

"Very well. Blodgette, I am going to show you some cards and ask you some questions. Answer by pointing to the proper card."

Blodgette glared at Dr. Morella and signed a few words.

"What's this?" she asked.

"Blodgette asked you to go," Gale said. "I think she's getting a little impatient."

"It will be only a few more minutes," the doctor assured.

You go. Blodgette repeated.

"I take she is still unreceptive?"

You go, please.

"She's being very polite about it," Gale said.

Markus turned to her.

"Blodgette, if you do this one last thing, I'll give you two whole cans of tomato paste, then I'll read you a story, and we'll both go swimming, okay?"

Blodgette's eyes literally flashed with the promise. She turned and prompted Dr. Morella to begin.

The questions were simple. Which card has more dots? Which of these is an animal? Which of these is a plant? She did quite well on most, though she only answered about half of the math questions. After each question, Dr. Morella took some notes.

"I think that will do."

"Okay," Markus said.

Blodgette tugged at his arm, trying to lead him inside to make good on his offer.

"Just a moment," he said. "When will we know the results?"

"Oh, immediately," she said, flipping back through her notes. "The enclosure is sufficient. I would recommend a better filtration system for the pond, but it is within acceptable levels. She is ahead of the curve on intelligence. I'm intrigued by this sign language experiment. She seems to have taken to it. She's behind in height and weight, though the weight may be in part to the thinness of the metal. Were she to have matured in a proper oven she would have a higher proportion of masonry. Her skin troubles me, as does the seemingly permanent deformation of both her tail and her neck. If you've kept proper notes, and it seems Ms. Dekker has done an exceptional job of it, then she has made improvements in all areas since she came under your care. Overall, she is on a good trajectory, and you have the facilities to raise her properly. If she were to be socialized properly, which simply requires careful introduction with a few more individuals over time, then I see no reason why SCOPE would not be an adequate home for Blodgette for the next two to four years, after which she will be more capable of making her own decisions regarding permanent residency."

Markus smiled.

"Then she can stay?"

Dr. Santino cleared her throat. "If you would be good enough to remove the *Structophis gastrignae* from the area."

"Why?" Markus said flatly.

"I think you know why."

The statement came like a punch to the gut. It showed on their faces. Blodgette glanced back and forth between them.

Why sad?

"We, uh… We should go inside now, Blodgette," Markus said, taking her by the hand.

She shook it off.

Why sad?

"Don't worry about it. I'll tell you later. Gale just has to—"

Blodgette stomped her foot.

I go?

Markus paused for a moment.

"Yeah," he said, finally. "You're going."

"Mr. Spiros, I'd asked you to take her aside for a *reason*," Dr. Morella said. "I was hoping to spare the creature any anxiety in the short term."

"She figured it out on her own," he snapped. "I'm not going to *lie* to her for you. So you may as well come out and say why you made that decision, because based upon all you've said, I can't figure out why. And she deserves to know."

"There was never any chance of her staying here," Dr. Morella said coldly. "Regardless of what the courts have decided, it is not lost upon *me* that your acquisition of Blodgette was the result of a criminal act. Whether it was the work of Dimitrios Spiros or the antique store from which he purchased the egg, Blodgette's presence here is illegitimate. And the amount of neglect evident in her emergence, one of the most crucial moments in a *Structophis gastrignae*'s development, is inexcusable. Permanent damage has been done, even if it appears to be superficial for the most part. To continue to leave her in the care of the individual at fault would be irresponsible."

No. Blodgette said with a stomp of her foot.

"Dr. Morella, my uncle is an idiot, I'll grant you that. But this whole place is only *bankrolled* by him. Every bit of care that's been given has been given by Gale and I. And you've said it yourself, she's done nothing but improve."

You go. Blodgette signed, stomping her foot again. *I stay.*

"She wants to stay," Markus added.

"And a child, if given the choice, would eat only candy. Sometimes we must impose our will upon a creature for its own good."

"Is there any chance I can go with her?" he asked.

The doctor scoffed. "The entire purpose of the move would be to keep her *away* from the individuals responsible for endangering her."

Safe here. Mom good. Wind good. You bad. You go. I stay.

"This would all be so much simpler to resolve if you could understand American Sign Language," Gale said. "She is telling you off, but good."

"If you'll take Blodgette inside, I'll discuss what needs to be done with Ms. Dekker."

Markus crossed his arms.

"No."

"This isn't up to you, Mr. Spiros."

"Dr. Morella, if you came here and told me Blodgette was terribly sick and needed to be taken away, then I'd have rushed her out the door with you. If you found that this place wouldn't be healthy for her, then I'd have downright demanded she be moved somewhere more appropriate. If she was getting worse then, again, take her away. But she's doing great."

"That doesn't change anything. I cannot allow such a precious creature to remain with people who would engage in such unscrupulous activities."

"My great-uncle did something he shouldn't have. That's not my fault, and that's not Blodgette's fault. We both know she's at a point in life where she needs someone to trust to help her grow. Do you have any doubt in your mind that she trusts me?"

"You can be replaced with time and care."

"And what happens between then and now? How much damage are you willing to do just to punish my uncle for what he did?"

Dr. Morella was briefly taken aback.

"You can't answer, can you? Because if you don't want to hurt her, then you know that you can't separate us. And if you *still* want to separate us, then you can't claim that you have her best interests at heart."

You bad, Blodgette signed.

She crossed her arms and huffed. Markus continued.

"When I first met Blodgette, I did a lot more thinking about me than I did about her. But that's changed. Blodgette's my responsibility. I take it very seriously. So if you want to take her away from me, you're going to need handcuffs, and you're going to have to watch what it does to her."

Dr. Morella was silent for a long time.

"Well," she said. "I certainly do not doubt your dedication to Blodgette."

A leaden silence hung in the air. It was only broken by the subtle shuffle of Blodgette's feet as she placed herself more directly in Dr. Morella's line of sight.

I stay? Blodgette asked.

"She's asking if she can stay."

Dr. Morella remained silent. Now it was Blodgette whose eyes she chose to avoid. The dragon was far less willing to endure such treatment. Blodgette clapped her mitts twice and repeated the sign.

I stay?

"Provisionally. *Extremely provisionally.*"

Blodgette blinked and turned to Gale.

I stay?

"Yes," Gale said with a sigh of relief.

Blodgette chirped triumphantly and swept first Markus, then Gale into a group hug.

"We will be watching you closely. And in the coming months you'll have to prepare her for a trip to meet another *Structophis*. It is not uncommon for *Structophis* to acclimate to a human society without much contact with others of their kind. For species preservation purposes, it is best to acclimate them to one another at an early age."

"Right. Fine," Markus groaned from within Blodgette's grip.

"I'll show myself out."

Dr. Morella marched out of the enclosure.

"Blodgette. You can let go," Markus said.

The dragon reluctantly did so, letting them drop to the ground. Gale was permitted to climb to her feet on her own and dust herself off. Markus, instead, was hauled off the ground by his hand and led into the shelter. It was rather spartan, with little more than a platform for her to sleep on and some additional flowers and plants. The one exception was the bookshelf against one corner. It was well stocked with storybooks, and a chair sat beside it along with a reading light.

She sat him down and pulled a well-worn book from the top shelf. After handing it to him, she thumped down on the ground to eagerly await what would probably be the twentieth read-through of the story.

Markus clicked on the light and thumbed the book open to the first page. It wasn't until he tried to read it, though, that he realized just how misty his vision had become.

"I guess I was a little worked up back there," he said, rubbing his eyes.

He blinked away the last of his tears and looked to Blodgette. She gave him a grin.

Thanks, Mom.

Blodgette illustrated by Chandra Free - Spookychan

From The Author

Thank you for reading! If you liked this story, or perhaps if you found it lacking, I'd love to hear from you. You can find me on-line at my website, bookofdeacon.com. For **free stories** and important updates, join my newsletter.

Discover other titles by Joseph R. Lallo:

The Free-Wrench – Steampunk Adventure Series:
Book 1: *Free-Wrench*
Book 2: *Skykeep*
Book 3: *Ichor Well*
Book 4: *The Calderan Problem*
Book 5: *Cipher Hill*
Book 6: *Contaminant Six*
Free Wrench Collection: Volume 1
Free Wrench Collection: Volume 2

The Shards of Shadow Series:
Book 1: *A Traitor in the Shadows*
Book 2: *The Prison of Shadows*
Book 3: *The Balance of Shadows*

The Greater Lands Series:
Book 1: *The Bygone Dagger*
Book 2: *The Bygone Archive*
Book 3: *The Bygone Mask*
Book 4: *The Bygone Caper*
Book 5: *The Bygone Plague*
Book 6: *The Bygone Way*

Other Stories:
Between
Fallen Empire: Rogue Derelict
Top Level Player
The Other Eight
Structophis
Between
Paradoxes and Dragons: Volume 1
Paradoxes and Dragons: Volume 2